BEAUTY
AND
SADNESS

BEAUTY
AND
SADNESS

Yasunari Kawabata

Translated from the Japanese by
HOWARD HIBBETT

Alfred A. Knopf *New York 1975*

THIS IS A BORZOI BOOK
PUBLISHED BY ALFRED A. KNOPF, INC.

Copyright © 1975 by Alfred A. Knopf, Inc.
All rights reserved under International
and Pan-American Copyright Conventions.
Published in the United States by Alfred A. Knopf, Inc.,
New York, and simultaneously in Canada by Random
House of Canada Limited, Toronto. Distributed
by Random House, Inc., New York. Originally
published in Japan as *Utsukushisa To Kanashimi To*
by Chuo koronsha, Tokyo. Copyright © 1961, 1962,
1963, 1964, 1965, by Yasunari Kawabata.

LIBRARY OF CONGRESS CATALOGING IN PUBLICATION DATA

Kawabata, Yasunari, Date.
Beauty and sadness.
Translation of Utsukushisa to kanashimi to.
I. Title.
PZ3.K1775Be3   [PL832.A9]   895.6′3′4   74-21281
ISBN 0-394-46055-3

Manufactured in the United States of America

FIRST AMERICAN EDITION

K179b

TEMPLE
BELLS

Five swivel chairs were ranged along the other side of the observation car of the Kyoto express. Oki Toshio noticed that the one on the end was quietly revolving with the movement of the train. He could not take his eyes from it. The low armchairs on his side of the car did not swivel.

Oki was alone in the observation car. Slouched deep in his armchair, he watched the end chair turn. Not that it kept turning in the same direction, at the same speed: sometimes it went a little faster, or a little slower, or even stopped and began turning in the opposite direction. To look at that one revolving chair, wheeling before him in the empty car, made him feel lonely. Thoughts of the past began flickering through his mind.

It was the twenty-ninth of December. Oki was going to Kyoto to hear the New Year's Eve bells.

For how many years had he heard the tolling of those

bells over the radio? How long ago had the broadcasts begun? Probably he had listened to them every year since then, and to the commentary by various announcers, as they picked up the sound of famous old bells from temples all around the country. During the broadcast the old year was giving way to the new, so the commentaries tended to be florid and emotional. The deep booming note of a huge Buddhist temple bell resounded at leisurely intervals, and the lingering reverberations held an awareness of the old Japan and of the flow of time. After the bells of the northern temples came the bells in Kyushu, but every New Year's Eve ended with the Kyoto bells. Kyoto had so many temples that sometimes the mingled sounds of a host of different bells came over the radio.

At midnight his wife and daughter might still be bustling about, preparing holiday delicacies in the kitchen, straightening up the house, or perhaps getting their kimonos ready or arranging flowers. Oki would sit in the dining room and listen to the radio. As the bells rang he would look back at the departing year. He always found it a moving experience. Some years that emotion was violent or painful. Sometimes he was racked by sorrow and regret. Even when the sentimentality of the announcers repelled him, the tolling of the bells echoed in his heart. For a long time he had been tempted by the thought of being in Kyoto one New Year's Eve to hear the living sound of those old temple bells.

That had come to mind again this year end, and he had impulsively decided to go to Kyoto. He had also been stirred by a defiant wish to see Ueno Otoko again after all these years, and to listen to the bells with her. Otoko had not written to him since she had moved to Kyoto, but by now she had established herself there as a painter in the classical Japanese tradition. She was still unmarried.

Because it was on impulse, and he disliked making reservations, Oki had simply gone to Yokohama Station and boarded the observation car of the Kyoto express. Near the holidays the train might be crowded, but he knew the porter and counted on getting a seat from him.

Oki found the Kyoto express convenient, since it left Tokyo and Yokohama early in the afternoon, arriving at Kyoto in the evening, and also left in early afternoon on its way back. He always made his trips to Kyoto on this train. Most of the girl attendants in the first-class cars knew him by sight.

Once aboard, he was surprised to find the car empty. Perhaps there were never many passengers on the twenty-ninth of December. It might be crowded again by the thirty-first.

As he kept watching the end chair turn, Oki began to think of fate. Just then the porter brought tea.

"Am I all alone?" Oki asked.

"Only five or six passengers today, sir."

"Will it be full on New Year's Day?"

"No, sir, it usually isn't. Is that when you're coming back?"

"I'm afraid so."

"I won't be on duty myself, but I'll see that you're taken care of."

"Thank you."

After the porter left, Oki looked around the car and saw a pair of white leather valises at the foot of the last armchair. They were square and rather slender, in a new style. The white leather was flecked with pale brownish dots; it was a kind unobtainable in Japan. Also, there was a large leopard-skin handbag on the chair. The owners of the luggage must be Americans. Probably they were in the dining car.

Woods flowed by in a thick, warm-looking haze outside the window. Far above the haze, white clouds were bathed in a shimmering light that seemed to radiate up from the earth. But as the train went on, the whole sky cleared. The sunlight slanting in the windows reached all across the car. As they passed a pine-covered mountain he could see that the ground was strewn with dry pine needles. A clump of bamboo had yellowed leaves. On the ocean side sparkling waves surged in to shore against a black cape.

Two middle-aged American couples came back from the dining car and, as soon as they could see Mt. Fuji, past Numazu, stood at the windows eagerly taking photographs. By the time Fuji was completely visible, down to the fields at its base, they seemed tired of photographing and had turned their backs to it.

The winter day was already ending. Oki let his eyes follow the dull silver-gray line of a river, and then looked up into the setting sun. For a long while the last bright chilly rays streamed through an arc-shaped cleft in the black clouds, before disappearing. The lights were on in

the car, and suddenly all the swivel chairs wheeled halfway around. But only the one on the end kept turning.

When he arrived in Kyoto, Oki went directly to the
Miyako Hotel. He asked for a quiet room, with the
thought that Otoko might come to see him. The elevator
seemed to rise six or seven floors; but since the hotel was
built in steps upward along a steep slope of the Eastern
Hills, the long corridor he followed led back to a ground-
floor wing. The rooms along the corridor were as silent
as if there were no other guests. A little after ten o'clock
he began hearing clamorous foreign voices all around
him. Oki asked the floor boy about it.

There were two families, he was told, with twelve children between them. The children not only shouted at
each other within their rooms but romped up and down
the corridor. Why, when the hotel seemed almost empty,
had they sandwiched him in between such noisy guests?
Oki restrained his annoyance, thinking the children
would soon go to sleep. But the noise went on and on,
perhaps because they were keyed up by the trip. What
especially grated on his ears was the sound of their footsteps running along the corridor. Finally he got out of
bed.

The loud chattering in a foreign language made Oki
feel all the more lonely. That revolving chair in the observation car, turning by itself, came before him. It was
as if he saw his own loneliness silently turning round and
round within his heart.

Oki had come to Kyoto to hear the New Year's Eve
bells and to see Ueno Otoko, but he wondered once

again which had been his real reason. Of course he was not sure he could see her. Yet were not the bells merely a pretext, and the chance of seeing her something he had long desired? He had come to Kyoto hoping to listen to the temple bells with Otoko. It had seemed a not unreasonable hope. But a gulf of many years lay between them. Though she had remained unmarried, it was quite possible that she would refuse to see an old lover, to accept an invitation from him.

"No, she's not like that," Oki muttered to himself. Still, he did not know how she might have changed.

It seemed that Otoko was living in a guest house on the grounds of a certain temple, along with a girl who was her protégée. Oki had come across a photograph of her in an art magazine. It was not a cottage, but a sizable house, with a large sitting room that she used as a studio. There was even a fine old garden. The photograph showed Otoko with brush in hand, bending over to work on a painting, but the line of her profile was unmistakable. Her figure was as slender as ever. Even before his old memories were awakened, he felt a stab of guilt at having robbed her of the possibility of marriage and motherhood. Obviously no one else would feel as he did about that photograph. To people who glanced at it in the magazine it would be merely the portrait of a woman artist who had gone to live in Kyoto and had become a typical Kyoto beauty.

Oki had thought he would telephone her the next day, if not that night, or drop in at her house. But in the morning, after being awakened by his neighbors' children, he began to feel hesitant, and decided to send her a special-delivery letter. As he sat at the writing desk staring perplexedly at a blank sheet of hotel stationery he decided that he need not see her, that it would be enough to hear the bells alone and then go back.

Oki had been aroused early by the children, but once the two foreign families went out he fell asleep again. It was almost eleven when he awakened.

Slowly tying his necktie, he suddenly recalled Otoko saying: "I'll tie it for you. Let me. . . . " She was fifteen, and those had been her first words after he had taken her virginity. Oki himself had not spoken. There was nothing he could say. He had been holding her tenderly close, stroking her hair, but he could not bring himself to speak. Then she had slipped out of his arms and begun to dress. He got up, put on his shirt, and started to tie his tie. She was looking up into his face, her eyes moist and shining, but not tearful. He avoided those eyes. Even when he had kissed her, earlier, Otoko had kept her eyes wide open until he pressed them shut with his lips.

There was a sweet, girlish ring in her voice as she asked to tie his tie. Oki felt a wave of relief. What she said was completely unexpected. Perhaps she was trying to escape from herself, rather than to indicate forgiveness, but she handled his necktie gently, though she seemed to be having trouble with it.

"Do you know how?" Oki asked.

"I think so. I used to watch my father."

Her father had died when Otoko was eleven.

Oki dropped into a chair and held Otoko facing him

on his lap, lifting his chin to make it easier for her. She crouched slightly toward him, several times undoing the tie and beginning over again. Then she slipped off his lap, trailing her fingers along his right shoulder, and gazed at the necktie. "There you are, Sonny-boy. Will that do?" Oki got up and went to the mirror. The knot was perfect. He rubbed the palm of his hand roughly across his face, with its faint oily film of sweat. He could hardly look at himself after having violated such a young girl. In the mirror he saw her face approaching. Startled by its fresh, poignant beauty, Oki turned round to her. She touched his shoulder, nestled her face against his chest, and said: "I love you."

It had also seemed strange that a fifteen-year-old girl should call a man twice her age "Sonny-boy."

That was twenty-four years ago. Now he was fifty-four. Otoko must be thirty-nine.

After his bath Oki had switched on the radio and learned that Kyoto had had a light freeze. The forecast said that the mild winter would probably continue over the holidays.

Oki breakfasted on toast and coffee in his room, and arranged to hire a car. Unable to make up his mind to call on Otoko, he decided to have the driver take him out to Mt. Arashi. From the car window he saw that the familiar, softly rounded low hills to the north and west, though some of them were in feeble sunlight, had the chilly drabness of a Kyoto winter. It looked as if the day were already ending. Oki got out of the car just before the

Togetsu Bridge, but instead of crossing it walked up the road along the river toward Kameyama Park.

At the end of the year even Mt. Arashi, so alive with tourists from spring till fall, had become a deserted landscape. The ancient mountain lay there before him, utterly still. The deep pool of the river at its base was a limpid green. In the distance echoed the sound of logs being loaded onto trucks from rafts along the bank. The mountainside descending to the river was the famous view, he supposed, but now it was in shadow except for a band of sunlight over the shoulder of Mt. Arashi that sloped toward the upper reaches of the river.

Oki had intended to have a quiet lunch by himself near Mt. Arashi. He had visited two restaurants there before. One of them was not far from the bridge, but its gate was closed. It seemed unlikely that people would come all the way out to this lonely mountain at the end of the year. Oki walked on along the river at a leisurely pace, wondering if the little rustic restaurant upstream would also be closed. He could always go back to the city for lunch. When he climbed the worn stone steps up to the restaurant, a girl turned him away, saying everyone had gone to Kyoto. How many years ago had it been, in the season for bamboo shoots, that he ate those young shoots in bonito broth here? He went back down to the road, and noticed an old woman sweeping leaves from a flight of low stone steps that led up to another restaurant next door. He asked if it was open, and she told him she thought so. Oki paused beside her for a moment, remarking how quiet it was. "Yes, you can hear people talking all the way across the river," she said.

The restaurant, buried in a hillside grove, had a thick, damp-looking old thatched roof and a dark entryway. One would hardly take it for a restaurant. In front, a stand of bamboo pressed in on it. The trunks of four or five splendid red pines towered beyond the thatched roof. Oki was shown into a private room, but there seemed to be no one else around. Just outside the glass sliding doors were red *aoki* berries. He saw a single aza-iea flower blooming out of season. *Aoki* shrubs and bamboos and the red pines blocked his view, but through the leaves he could glimpse a deep, clear jade-green pool in the river. All of Mt. Arashi was as still as that pool of water.

Oki sat at the *kotatsu,* both elbows propped on the low quilt-covered table over a warm charcoal brazier. He could hear a bird singing. The sound of logs being loaded on trucks echoed through the valley. From somewhere off in the Western Hills came the plaintive, lingering whistle of a train entering or leaving a tunnel. He was reminded of the thin cry of a newborn baby. . . . At sixteen, in the seventh month of carrying his child, Otoko had given birth. The baby was a girl.

Nothing could be done to save it, and Otoko never saw the baby. When it died, the doctor advised against letting her know too soon.

"Mr. Oki, I want you to tell her," Otoko's mother had said. "I'm apt to burst out crying, the poor thing having to go through all this, when she's still such a child."

For the time being Otoko's mother had suppressed her anger and resentment toward him. Her daughter was all she had, and once her daughter was pregnant, even by a man with a wife and child of his own, she no longer dared revile him. Her spirit failed, though it had seemed even stronger than Otoko's. She had to rely on Oki to see that the child was born in secret, and to arrange for its care afterward. Then too, Otoko, nervous and high-strung in pregnancy, had threatened to kill herself if her mother criticized him.

When he came back to her bedside, Otoko looked at him with the gentle eyes, drained of feeling, of a newly delivered mother. But soon tears welled up in the corners of her eyes. She must have guessed, Oki thought. The tears flowed uncontrollably. As one of the streams went toward her ear, he hastily dabbed at it. She grasped his hand, and for the first time broke into audible sobs. She wept and sobbed as if a dam had burst.

"It's dead, isn't it? The baby's dead, it's dead!"

She was writhing in anguish, and Oki held her tight, pinning her body down. He could feel one of her small, youthful breasts—small, but swollen with milk—against his arm.

Her mother came in and called to Otoko. Perhaps she had been just outside.

Oki kept his arms around her.

"I can't breathe," she said. "Let me go."

"Will you lie still? You won't move?"

"I'll lie still."

He released her, and her shoulders sagged. New tears began to seep through her closed eyelids.

"Mother, are you going to cremate it?"

There was no answer.

"Such a tiny baby?"

Again her mother did not answer.

"Didn't you say I had jet-black hair when I was born?"

"Yes, jet black."

"Was my baby's hair like that? Mother, could you save some for me?"

"I don't know, Otoko." Her mother hesitated, and then blurted out: "You can have another one!" She turned away frowning, as if she wanted to swallow her own words.

Had not Otoko's mother, and even Oki himself, secretly hoped the child would never see the light of day? Otoko had given birth in a dingy little clinic on the outskirts of Tokyo. Oki felt a sharp pang at the thought that the baby's life might have been saved if it had been cared for in a good hospital. He had taken her to the clinic alone. Her mother could not endure it. The doctor was a middle-aged man with the reddened face of an alcoholic. The young nurse looked accusingly at Oki. Otoko was wearing a kimono—still of a childish cut— with a matching cloak of cheap, dark-blue silk.

The image of a premature baby with jet-black hair appeared before Oki, there at Mt. Arashi over twenty years later. It flickered in the wintry groves of trees, and in the depths of the green pool. He clapped his hands to summon the waitress. Clearly no guests had been expected, and it would take a long time to prepare his meal. A waitress brought tea and stayed chatting on and on, as if to keep him entertained.

One of her stories was about a man bewitched by a badger. They had found him splashing along in the river at dawn, screaming for help. He was floundering in the shallows under the Togetsu Bridge, where you could easily climb up on the bank. It seems that after he was rescued and came to his senses, he told them he had been wandering around the mountain like a sleepwalker from about ten o'clock the night before—and the next thing he knew he was in the river.

Finally the kitchen had the first course ready: slices of fresh silver carp. Oki sipped a little sake with it.

As he left he looked up again at the heavy thatched roof. Its mossy, decaying charm appealed to him, but the mistress of the restaurant explained that, being under the trees, it never really got a chance to dry out. It was not very old, less than ten years ago they had put on new thatching. A half moon gleamed in the sky just beyond the roof. It was three-thirty. As Oki went down the river road he watched kingfishers skimming low over the water. He could see the colors of their wings.

Near Togetsu Bridge he got into the car again, intending to go to the Adashino graveyard. In the gathering winter twilight the forest of tombstones and Jizo figures would soothe his feelings. But when he saw how dusky it was in the bamboo grove at the entrance to the Gio Temple he had the driver turn back. He decided to stop in at the Moss Temple and then go to the hotel. The temple garden was empty except for a couple who looked like honeymooners. Dry pine needles lay scattered over the moss, and reflections of trees in the pond shifted as he walked along. On the way back to the hotel, the Eastern Hills ahead glowed in the orange light of the setting sun.

After warming himself with a bath, he looked for Ueno Otoko's number in the phone book. A young woman answered, no doubt her protégée, and immediately turned the telephone over to Otoko.

"Hello."

"This is Oki." He waited. "It's Oki. Oki Toshio."

"Yes. It's been such a long time." She spoke with the soft Kyoto drawl.

He was not sure how to begin, so he went on quickly to avoid embarrassing her, as if he were calling on impulse.

"I came to hear the New Year's Eve bells in Kyoto."

"The bells?"

"Won't you listen to them with me?"

She made no reply, even when he repeated his question. Probably she was too surprised to know what to say.

"Did you come alone?" she asked, after a long pause.

"Yes. Yes, I'm alone."

Again Otoko was silent.

"I'm going back New Year's morning—I just wanted to hear the bells toll out the old year with you. I'm not so young anymore, you know. How many years is it since the last time we met? It's been so long I suppose I wouldn't dare ask to see you without an occasion like this."

There was no answer.

"May I call for you tomorrow?"

"No, don't," Otoko said a little hastily. "I'll come for *you*. At eight o'clock . . . perhaps that's early, so let's say around nine, at your hotel. I'll make a reservation somewhere."

Oki had hoped for a leisurely dinner with her, but nine o'clock would be after dinner. Still, he was glad she had agreed. The Otoko of his old memories had come to life again.

He spent the next day alone in his hotel room, morning till evening. That it was the last day of the year made the time seem even longer. There was nothing to do. He had friends in Kyoto, but it was not a day when he cared to see them. Nor did he want anyone to know he was in the city. Although he knew a good many restaurants with tempting Kyoto specialties, he decided to have a simple, businesslike dinner at the hotel. So the last day of the old year was filled with memories of Otoko. As the same memories kept recurring to his mind they became increasingly vivid. Events of over twenty years ago were more alive to him than those of yesterday.

Too far from the window to see the street below, Oki sat looking out over the rooftops at the Western Hills. Compared with Tokyo, Kyoto was such a small, intimate city that even the Western Hills were close at hand. As he gazed, a translucent pale gold cloud above the hills turned a chilly ashen color, and it was evening.

What were memories? What was the past that he remembered so clearly? When Otoko moved to Kyoto with her mother, Oki was sure they had parted. Yet had they, really? He could not escape the pain of having spoiled her life, possibly of having robbed her of every chance for happiness. But what had she thought of him as she spent all those lonely years? The Otoko of his memories was the most passionate woman he had ever known. And did not the vividness even now of those memories mean that she was not separated from him? Although he had never lived here, the lights of Kyoto in the evening had a nostalgic appeal for him. Perhaps every Japanese would feel that way. Still, Otoko was here. Restless, he took a bath, changed into fresh clothing, and walked up and down the room, stopping occasionally to look at himself in the mirror as he waited for her.

It was twenty past nine when a call from the lobby announced Miss Ueno.

"Tell her I'll be down in a moment," Oki answered. Or should I have had her come up here? he said to himself.

Otoko was nowhere to be seen in the spacious lobby. A young girl approached and inquired politely if he was Mr. Oki. She said Miss Ueno had asked her to call for him.

"Oh?" He tried to be casual. "That's very kind of you."

Having expected only Otoko, he felt that she had eluded him. The vivid memories of her that had filled his day seemed to dissipate.

Oki was silent for a time after getting into the car the girl had waiting for them. Then he asked: "Are you Miss Ueno's pupil?"

"Yes."

"And you're living with her?"

"Yes. There's a maid too."

"I suppose you're from Kyoto."

"No, Tokyo. But I fell in love with Miss Ueno's work and came chasing after her, so she took me in." Oki looked at the girl. The moment she spoke to him at the hotel he had been aware of her beauty and now he noticed how lovely she was in profile. She had a longish slender neck, and charmingly shaped ears. Altogether, she was disturbingly beautiful. But she spoke quietly, in a rather reserved manner. He wondered if she knew what was between him and Otoko, something that had happened before she was born. Suddenly he asked: "Do you always wear a kimono?"

"No, I'm not so proper," she said, a little more easily. "At home I usually wear slacks. Miss Ueno said I should dress for the holiday, because New Year's Day would come while we were out." Apparently she was also to listen to the bells with them. He realized that Otoko was avoiding being alone with him.

The car went up through Maruyama Park toward the Chionin Temple. Awaiting them in a private room at an elegant old tea house were two young apprentice geisha, besides Otoko herself. Again he was caught by surprise. Otoko was sitting alone at the *kotatsu*, her knees under its coverlet; the two geisha sat across from each other at an open brazier. The girl who had brought him knelt at the doorway and bowed.

Otoko drew herself away from the *kotatsu* to greet him. "It's been such a long time," she said. "I thought you might like to be near the Chionin bell, but I'm afraid they can't offer anything elaborate here, they're really closed for the holidays."

All Oki could do was thank her for going to so much trouble. But to have two geisha, besides her pupil! He could not even hint at the past they had shared, or let the way he looked at her betray it. His telephone call yesterday must have left her so upset and worried that she had decided to invite the geisha. Did her reluctance to be alone with him indicate the state of her feelings toward him? He had thought so the moment he was face to face with her. But at that first glance he felt he was still living within her. Probably the others did not notice. Or perhaps they did, since the girl was with her every day, and the geisha, though very young, were women of the pleasure quarter. Of course none of them showed the least sign of it.

Otoko remained at one side, between the geisha, and had Oki sit at the *kotatsu*. Then she had her pupil take the seat opposite him. She seemed to be avoiding him again.

"Miss Sakami, have you introduced yourself to Mr. Oki?" she asked lightly, and went on, as if formally presenting her: "This is Sakami Keiko, who's staying with me. She may not look it, but she's a bit crazy."

"Oh, Miss Ueno!"

"She does abstract paintings in a style all her own. They're so passionate they often seem a little mad. But I'm quite taken with them; I envy her. You can see her tremble as she paints."

A waitress brought sake and tidbits. The two geisha poured for them.

"I had no idea I'd be listening to the bells in this sort of company," said Oki.

"I thought it might be pleasanter with young people. It's lonely, when the bell tolls and you're another year older." Otoko kept her eyes down. "I often wonder why I've gone on living so long."

Oki remembered that two months after the death of her baby Otoko took an overdose of sleeping medicine. Had she also remembered? He had rushed to her side as soon as he learned of it. Her mother's efforts to get Otoko to leave him had brought on the suicide attempt, but she sent for him nevertheless. Oki stayed at their house to help take care of her. Hour after hour he massaged her thighs, swollen and hard from massive injections. Her mother went in and out of the kitchen bringing hot steamed towels. Otoko lay nude under a light kimono. Still only sixteen, she had very slender thighs, and the injections made them swell up grotesquely. Sometimes when he pressed hard his hands slipped down to her inner thighs. While her mother was out of the room he wiped away the ugly discharge oozing between them. His own tears of pity and bitter shame fell on them, and he swore to himself that he would save her, that he would never part from her, come what might.

Otoko's lips had turned purple. He heard her mother sobbing in the kitchen, and found her crouched before the stove.

"She's dying!"

"You've done all you could," he told her.

"And so have you," she said, gripping his hand.

He stayed by Otoko's side for three days without sleeping, until she finally opened her eyes. She writhed and moaned in pain, pawing frantically at herself. Then her glaring eyes seemed to fix on him. "No, no! Go away!"

Two doctors had done their utmost for her, but Oki felt that his own devoted nursing had helped to save her life.

Probably Otoko's mother had not told her everything he had done. But to him it was unforgettable. More vivid than the memory of her body lying in his embrace was that of her naked thighs as he massaged her back to life. He could see them even as she sat there with him waiting to hear the temple bell.

No sooner had anyone filled her sake cup than Otoko drained it. Evidently she knew how to hold her liquor. One of the geisha said it took an hour to give the bell all one hundred and eight strokes. Both geisha were in ordinary kimonos, not turned out for a party. They were not wearing dangling butterfly obi, and instead of fancy flowered hairpins they had only pretty combs in their hair. Both of them seemed to be friends of Otoko, but Oki could not understand why they had come dressed so casually. As he drank, listening to the frivolous chatter of their soft Kyoto voices, his heart lightened. Otoko had been quite astute. She had avoided being alone with him, but she might very well have wanted to calm her own emotions for this unexpected reunion. Even to sit here together created a current of feeling that flowed back and forth between them.

The great bell of the Chionin tolled.

A hush fell over the room. The worn old bell sounded almost cracked, but its reverberations hung on and on. After an interval, it tolled again. It seemed to be very near.

"We're too close," said Otoko. "I was told this would be a good place to hear the Chionin bell, but I think it might have sounded better from a little farther away, somewhere by the river, maybe."

Oki slid back the paper screen from a window and saw that the bell tower was just below the small garden of the tea house. "It's right over there," he said. "You can see them striking it."

"We really are too close," Otoko repeated.

"No, this is fine," Oki said. "I'm glad to be so near for once, after hearing it over the radio every New Year's Eve." Yet there was indeed something lacking. Dark shadowy figures had gathered in front of the bell tower. He closed the screen and went back to the *kotatsu.* As the bell tolled on he stopped straining to listen to it, and then he heard a sound that only a magnificent old bell could produce, a sound that seemed to roar forth with all the latent power of a distant world.

After leaving the tea house they walked up to the Gion

Shrine for the traditional New Year ceremony. Many were already on their way back from it, swinging the fire-tipped cords they had lighted at the shrine. According to long custom, that fire would light the stove for cooking holiday dishes.

EARLY SPRING

Oki was standing on a low hill, his gaze held by the purple sunset. He had been at his desk since half past one that afternoon, and had left the house to take a walk after finishing an installment of a serial for a newspaper. He lived in the hilly northern outskirts of Kamakura, and his house was across the valley. The glow spread high in the western sky. The richness of the purple made him wonder if there might be a thin bank of clouds. A purple sunset was most unusual. There were subtle gradations of color from dark to light, as if blended by trailing a wide brush across wet rice paper. The softness of the purple implied the coming of spring. At one place the haze was pink. That seemed to be where the sun was setting.

He recalled that on his way back from Kyoto on New Year's Day the rails glinted crimson far into the distance in the rays of the setting sun. On one side was the sea.

As the rails curved into the shadow of the hills their crimson disappeared. The train entered a gorge, and suddenly it was evening. But the warm crimson of the rails had reminded him again of the past he had shared with Otoko. Although she had avoided being alone with him, that very fact made him feel that he was still alive within her. As they walked back from the Gion Shrine some drunken men in the crowds had accosted them and tried to touch the high-piled coiffures of the two young geisha. One seldom saw that kind of behavior in Kyoto. Oki walked beside the geisha to shield them, Otoko and her pupil following along a few steps behind.

The next day as he was about to board the train, still telling himself that Otoko could not be expected to come to the station, her pupil Sakami Keiko appeared.

"Happy New Year! Miss Ueno says she wanted to see you off, but she's had to make New Year's calls all morning, and this afternoon people are coming to see her. So I'm here in her place."

"That's very kind of you," Oki replied. Her beauty attracted attention among the few holiday travelers. "This is the second time I've troubled you."

"Not at all."

Keiko was wearing the same kimono as last night: a bluish figured satin with a design of plovers fluttering among scattered snowflakes. The plovers gave it color, but it was rather somber holiday finery for such a young girl.

"That's a handsome kimono. Did Miss Ueno paint the design?"

"No." She blushed faintly. "I did it myself, though it's not what I'd hoped." Actually the somber kimono brought out Keiko's disturbing beauty all the more strikingly. And there was a youthfulness in the decorative color harmonies and varied shapes of the plovers. Even the scattered snowflakes seemed to be dancing.

Saying it was from Otoko, she gave him several boxes of Kyoto delicacies to eat on the train.

During the few minutes the train waited in the station Keiko came over and stood at his window. As he saw her there framed in the window it occurred to him that, in her whole life, this might be the time when she was at her most beautiful. He had not known Otoko in the full flower of her youthful beauty. She was sixteen when they parted.

Oki opened his supper early, around four-thirty. It was an assortment of New Year's foods, including some small, perfectly formed rice balls. They seemed to express a woman's emotions. No doubt Otoko herself had made them for the man who had long ago destroyed her girlhood. Chewing the little bite-sized rice balls, he could feel her forgiveness in his very tongue and teeth. No, it was not forgiveness, it was love. Surely it was a love that still lived deep within her. All he knew of her years in Kyoto was that she had made her way alone, as a painter. Perhaps there had been other loves, other affairs. Yet he knew that what she felt for him was a young girl's desperate love. He himself had gone on to other women. But he had never loved again with such pain.

Delicious rice, he thought, wondering if it was grown

around Kyoto. He ate one little rice ball after another. They were seasoned exactly right, neither too salty nor too bland.

About two months after her suicide attempt Otoko had been hospitalized in a psychiatric ward, behind barred windows. He learned of it from her mother, but was not allowed to see her.

"You could look at her from the corridor," Otoko's mother had said, "but I wish you wouldn't. I'd hate to have you see the poor child now myself. And she'd be upset if she saw you."

"Do you think she'd recognize me?"

"Of course she would! Isn't it all because of you?"

Oki had no reply.

"But they say she hasn't gone crazy. The doctor tells me not to worry, she'll only be there a little while." Her mother gestured as if cradling a baby in her arms. "She often goes like this, wanting her baby. She's really pitiful."

Otoko left the hospital after some three months. Her mother came to talk to him.

"I know you have a wife and child, and Otoko must have known that too from the very beginning. So maybe you'll think *I'm* crazy, at my age, asking it of you. . . ." She was trembling, with tears in her downcast eyes. "Won't you please marry her?"

"I've been thinking about that," Oki said unhappily. There had been stormy scenes at home as well. His wife was then in her early twenties.

"You can just ignore me, as if I'm a little deranged too.

I'll never ask again. But I'm not saying right away. She can wait a few years, even five or six—she's the kind of girl who'll go on waiting whether I want her to or not. And she's only sixteen."

It occurred to him that Otoko's passionate temperament came from her mother.

Within a year Otoko's mother sold their house in Tokyo and took her daughter to live in Kyoto. Otoko transferred to a girls' high school there, dropping one grade behind. As soon as she was graduated from high school she entered an art school.

It was over twenty years later that they listened to the Chionin bell together, that she sent him a supper to eat on the train back to Tokyo. All her holiday foods seemed to be in the old Kyoto tradition, Oki thought, as he took the morsels up one by one in his chopsticks. Even breakfast at the hotel that morning had included a bowl of the traditional New Year's soup, for form's sake, but the true flavor of the holiday was in this supper. At home in Kamakura it would all be quite Westernized, the way it looked in the color photographs in women's magazines.

Someone in Otoko's position "had to make New Year's calls," as Keiko said, but she could at least have stolen ten or fifteen minutes to come to the station. She was keeping aloof from him again. But although he had been unable to say anything about it last night in the presence of the others, their past together seemed to create a current of feeling between them. It was true of this supper too.

As the train began to move Oki had tapped the window, lifted it slightly so that she could hear, and thanked Keiko again and invited her to visit him when she came to Tokyo. "You can easily find us, just ask at the North Kamakura Station. And send me a painting or two of yours, won't you? An abstract, the kind Miss Ueno calls a little mad."

"How embarrassing! Having Miss Ueno say a thing like that. . . . " For a moment there was an odd sparkle in her eyes.

"But doesn't she envy your ability?"

The train had stopped in the station only briefly, and his conversation with Keiko had been brief too.

Oki himself had never written an "abstract" novel, though some of his novels had an element of fantasy. Insofar as language diverged from everyday reality it might be thought of as abstract or symbolic, but he had always tried to suppress such tendencies in his writing. He had liked French symbolist poetry, as well as haiku and medieval Japanese poetry, but ever since he began writing he seemed to have been learning to use abstract, symbolic language to cultivate a concrete, realistic mode of expression. However, he had thought that by deepening this kind of expression he would eventually arrive at a symbolic quality.

But what, for example, was the relation between the Otoko in his novel and the real Otoko? It was hard to say.

Of all his novels, the one that had had the longest life, and was still widely read, was the one that told the story of his love affair with her. The publication of that novel had caused her further injury, eventually turning the eyes of the curious on her. Yet why had she now, decades later, gained the affection of so many readers?

Perhaps one should say that the Otoko in his novel, rather than the girl who was the model for the character, had gained the affection of his readers. It was not Otoko's own story, it was something he had written. He had added imaginative and fictional touches of his own, and a certain idealization. Leaving that aside, who could say which was the real Otoko—the one he had described, or the one she might have created in telling her own story?

Still, the girl in his novel was Otoko. The novel could not have existed without their love affair. And it was because of her that it continued to be so widely read. If he had never met her he would never have known such a love. To find a love like that, at thirty, might be taken as good luck or bad, he could not say which, but there was no doubt that it had given him a fortunate debut as an author.

Oki had called his novel *A Girl of Sixteen*. It was an ordinary, straightforward title, but in those days people thought it shocking that a teen-age schoolgirl should take a lover, have a premature baby, suffer a lapse of sanity. To Oki, her lover, it had not seemed shocking. And of course he had not written about it in that spirit, nor had he regarded her as strange. Like the title, the author's attitude was straightforward, and Otoko was depicted as a pure, ardent young girl. He had tried to bring to life his impression of her face, her figure, the way she moved. In short, he had poured all his fresh, youthful love into the book. Probably that was why it had been so successful. It was the tragic love story of a very young girl and a man himself still young but with a wife and child: only the beauty of it had been heightened, to the point that it was unmarred by any moral questioning.

In the days when he was secretly meeting Otoko, she once startled him by saying: "You're the kind who's always worrying about what other people think, aren't you? You ought to be bolder."

"I thought I was shameless enough. How about right now?"

"No, I'm not talking about us." She paused. "It's everything—you ought to be more yourself."

Oki reflected on himself, at a loss to reply. Long afterward her words stuck in his mind. He felt it was because she loved him that this child could see through his character and his life. He had gone on to indulge himself often enough, but whenever he began to worry about other people's opinions he remembered her words. He remembered her as she said them.

He had stopped caressing her for a moment. Otoko, perhaps thinking it was because of what she had said, nestled her face in the crook of his arm. Then she began to bite, harder and harder. Oki kept his arm still, bearing the pain. He could feel her tears on his skin.

"You're hurting me," he said, grasping her by the hair and drawing her away. Blood was oozing from the teeth marks in his arm. Otoko licked the wound.

"Hurt me too," she said. Oki gazed at her arm—truly the arm of a young girl—and ran his hand up it from the fingertips to the shoulder. He kissed her shoulder. She squirmed with pleasure.

It was not because she had said "You ought to be more yourself" that Oki wrote *A Girl of Sixteen,* but as he was writing it he remembered those words. Two years after he parted from her the novel was published. Otoko was living in Kyoto. Her mother must have left Tokyo because of his failure to respond to her appeal; probably she could no longer endure the sorrow that she shared with her daughter. What had they thought of his novel, of his winning success with a work that touched their lives so deeply? To be sure, no one brought up the question of the model for the heroine of the young author's novel. Only after Oki was in his fifties, and people were beginning to investigate his career, had it become known that the character was based on Otoko. That was after her mother had died, and by then Otoko had made a name for herself as a painter, and photographs of her with the caption "the heroine of *A Girl of Sixteen*" had begun to appear in magazines. He imagined that the photographs were used without her consent. Naturally she gave no interviews on the subject. Even when the novel first appeared Oki heard nothing from her or her mother about it.

The trouble had occurred in his own household. That was to be expected. Before their marriage Fumiko was a typist at a news agency, and so Oki had had his young bride type up all his writings. It was something of a lovers' game, the sweet togetherness of newlyweds, but there was more to it than that. When his work first appeared in a magazine he was astonished at the difference in effect between a pen-written manuscript and the tiny characters in print. However, as he became more experienced he began to anticipate the effect of his words on the printed page. Not that he wrote with that in mind, he never gave it a thought, but the gap between manuscript and published work disappeared. He had learned how to write for print. Even passages that seemed tedious or loose in manuscript would turn out to be tightly written. Perhaps that meant that he had learned his craft. He often told beginning novelists: "Get something in print, in a little magazine or anywhere. It's very different from manuscript—you'll be surprised how much you learn."

The present-day form of publication was printing in type. But he had had the opposite kind of surprise too. For example, he had always read *The Tale of Genji* in the small type of modern editions, but when he came across it in a handsome old block-printed edition it made an entirely different impression on him. What had it been like when they read it in those beautiful flowing manuscripts of the age of the Heian Court? A thousand years ago *The Tale of Genji* was a modern novel. It could never be read that way again, no matter how far *Genji* studies progressed. Still, the old edition gave a more intense pleasure than a modern one. Doubtless the same would be true of Heian poetry. As for later literature, Oki had tried reading Saikaku in facsimiles of the seventeenth-century block-print editions, not out of antiquarianism but because he wanted to come as close as he could to the original work. But to read contemporary novels in manuscript facsimile was sheer dilettantism; they were meant to be read in type print, not in a boring handwriting.

By the time he married Fumiko there was no longer any serious gap between his manuscripts and the printed versions, but since his wife was a typist he had her type them up for him. Typewritten manuscripts in Japanese were far closer to printing than handwritten ones. Then too, he knew that almost all Western manuscripts were either produced on the typewriter or typed up in clean copies. But the typescripts of Oki's novels, partly because he was not used to them, seemed colder and flatter than either the pen manuscripts or the final printed versions. Yet for that reason he could recognize their defects, and found it easier to make corrections and revisions. And so it had become customary for Fumiko to type up all his manuscripts.

Hence the problem of what to do with the manuscript of *A Girl of Sixteen.* To have Fumiko type it would be to cause her pain and humiliation. It would be cruel. When he met Otoko his wife was twenty-two and had just given birth to their son. Of course she suspected her husband's love affair. She would go out at night, carrying the baby on her back, and wander along the railroad tracks. Once, after she was gone for several hours, he discovered her in the garden leaning on the old plum tree, unwilling to return to the house. He had been out looking for her, and heard her sobbing as he came in the gate.

"What on earth are you doing? You'll make the baby catch cold."

It was mid-March, and still quite chilly. The baby did catch cold. It was hospitalized with a touch of pneumonia. Fumiko stayed at the hospital to look after it.

"It'll be convenient for you if he dies," she would say to him. "Then you'll have no trouble leaving me." Even so, Oki took advantage of his wife's absence to go to meet Otoko. The baby was saved.

The next year, when Otoko had her premature baby, Fumiko learned about it by coming across a letter from Otoko's mother. That so young a girl should have a baby was not in itself surprising, but Fumiko had never dreamed of such a thing. Railing at him, she flew into a passion and bit her tongue. When he saw blood trickling between her lips, Oki hastily forced her mouth open and stuck in his hand, until she began to choke and retch, and then go limp. His fingers were bleeding when he drew them out. At that Fumiko calmed down and set about bandaging his hand.

Before the novel was finished Fumiko had also found out that Otoko had broken off from him and gone to Kyoto. Having her type the manuscript would reopen the wounds of her jealousy and pain, but otherwise he would seem to be treating it as a secret. Oki was perplexed, but finally decided to give her the manuscript. For one thing, he wanted to make a full confession to her. She immediately read it through from beginning to end.

"I ought to have let you go," she said, paling. "I wonder why I didn't. Everybody who reads it will sympathize with Otoko."

"I didn't want to write about you."

"I know I can't be compared with your ideal woman."

"That's not what I meant."

"I was hideously jealous."

"Otoko is gone. You and I will be living together for a long, long time. But a lot of the Otoko in that book is pure fiction. For instance, I have no idea what she was like while she was in the hospital."

"That kind of fiction comes from love."

"I couldn't have written without it," said Oki abruptly. "Will you type this one for me too? I hate to ask you."

"I'll type it. A typewriter is just a machine, after all. I'll be part of the machine."

Of course Fumiko could not simply function mechanically. She seemed to make frequent mistakes—he often heard her tear up a sheet of paper. Sometimes she paused, and he could hear her weeping quietly. Since the house was so small, and the typewriter was in a corner of the cramped dining room next to his shabby study, he was very well aware of his wife's presence. It was hard to sit calmly at his desk.

Nevertheless, Fumiko said not a word about *A Girl of Sixteen.* She seemed to think a "machine" ought not to talk. The manuscript ran to some three hundred and fifty pages, and for all her experience would obviously take many days to complete. Soon she had become quite sallow and hollow-cheeked. She would sit staring nowhere, clinging to her typewriter as if possessed, her brows knitted grimly. Then one day before dinner she threw up a yellowish substance and slumped over. Oki went to stroke her back.

Gasping, she asked for water. There were tears in her red-rimmed eyes.

"I'm sorry. I shouldn't have had you type it," he said. "Though to try to keep this one book away from you . . . " Even if it had not destroyed their marriage, that wound too would have been slow to heal.

"I'm glad you did, anyway." Fumiko tried to smile. "I'm really exhausted. It's the first time I've typed anything this long all at once."

"The longer it is, the longer you're tortured. Maybe that's the fate of a novelist's wife."

"Thanks to your novel I've come to understand Otoko very well. As much as I've suffered from it, I can see that meeting her was a good thing for you."

"Didn't I tell you she's idealized?"

"I know. There aren't any lovely girls exactly like that. But I wish you'd written more about me! I wouldn't care if I'd come out a horrible, jealous shrew."

Oki found it hard to reply. "You were never that."

"You didn't know what was in my heart."

"I wasn't willing to expose all our family secrets."

"No, you were so wrapped up in that little Otoko you only wanted to write about her! I suppose you thought I would soil her beauty and dirty up your novel. But does a novel have to be so pretty?"

Even his reluctance to describe his wife's jealous rage

had invited a new outburst of jealousy. Not that he had omitted it altogether. Indeed, to have written so concisely of it might have strengthened the effect. But Fumiko seemed to feel frustrated that he had not gone into detail. He was baffled by his wife's psychology. How could she feel ignored? Since the novel was about his tragic love affair it was centered on Otoko. He had included without change a great many facts hitherto concealed from his wife. That was what had worried him most, but she seemed more hurt that he had written so little about her.

"I didn't like to use your jealousy that way," Oki said.

"Because you can't write about someone you don't love, someone you don't even hate? All the time I'm typing I keep wondering why I didn't let you go."

"You're talking nonsense again."

"I'm serious. Holding on to you was a crime. I'll probably regret it the rest of my life."

"Stop that!" He grasped her by the shoulders and shook her. Fumiko shuddered convulsively and again vomited something yellow. Oki released her.

"It's all right," she said. "I think it's . . . morning sickness."

"What!"

Fumiko put her hands to her face and wept aloud.

"Then you've got to take care of yourself. You ought to stop typing."

"No, I want to go on. There isn't much left, and it's just using my fingers."

She refused to listen to him. Within a week after finishing it she had a miscarriage. Apparently the cause was the emotional shock of the manuscript, rather than the typing itself. She was in bed for days, and her thick, soft hair, which she let hang in braids, thinned out a little. But her unpowdered, colorless face looked smooth and sleek. Being young, Fumiko suffered no great aftereffects from her miscarriage.

Oki put the manuscript away in his files, not wishing either to destroy it or to look at it again. Two lives were buried in darkness with this novel. Was it not ill-omened, considering Otoko's premature baby and Fumiko's miscarriage? Both husband and wife avoided mentioning the novel for a long while. At last Fumiko brought it up.

"Why don't you publish it? Are you worried about hurting me? When a woman's married to a novelist that sort of thing can't be helped. If you're worried about anyone, it ought to be Otoko." By that time in her recovery, Fumiko's skin seemed quite lustrous and pretty. Was it the marvel of youth? Even her appetite for her husband had become keener.

About the time *A Girl of Sixteen* was published, Fumiko became pregnant again.

A Girl of Sixteen was praised by the critics. Moreover, a great many readers liked it. Fumiko could scarcely have forgotten her jealousy, but she showed only pleasure at her husband's success. And it was this novel, reputedly the finest of his early writings, that continued to outsell all his other works. For Fumiko it had meant new clothes, even jewelry, to say nothing of helping to pay for the education of her son and daughter. Had she by now very nearly forgotten that all this was because of a young girl's affair with her husband? Did she accept the money as his normal income? At the least, was that long past tragic love, for her, no longer tragic?

Oki was by no means opposed to that, but it sometimes made him stop to think. Otoko, as model for the novel's heroine, had received no compensation. Nor had a word of complaint come either from her or from her mother. Unlike the painter or sculptor of a realistic portrait, he was able to enter his model's thoughts and feelings, to change her appearance as he pleased, to invent and to idealize out of his own imagination. Yet the girl was beyond doubt Otoko. He had freely poured out his youthful passion, without thinking of her predicament, or of the troubles that might lie ahead for an unmarried girl. No doubt it was his passion that had attracted readers, but possibly it had also become an obstacle to her marriage. The novel had brought him money and fame. It seemed that Fumiko's jealousy had been diverted, and perhaps the wound had healed. There was even a difference in the loss of their babies. Fumiko was still his wife; she had had a normal recovery from the miscarriage, and in due time she gave birth to a baby girl. The years passed, and the only person that never changed was the girl in the pages of his book. From a vulgar domestic point of view it was fortunate that he had not stressed Fumiko's wild jealousy, though that was possibly a weakness of the novel. But it was also what made it so readable, and his heroine so appealing.

Later, when people spoke of Oki's best works they

invariably began with *A Girl of Sixteen.* As a novelist, he found this depressing, and he would gloomily tell himself how much he disliked it. Still, the book did have the freshness of youth. And public taste supported by established critical opinion could hardly be swayed even by the author's objections. The work began to have a life of its own. But what had become of Otoko after her mother took her to Kyoto? The question preyed on his mind, partly because of the continuing life of the novel.

Only in recent years had Otoko made a name for herself as a painter. Until then he had heard nothing of her. He supposed she had married and was living an ordinary life, as indeed he hoped. But he found it hard to imagine of a girl with her temperament. Did that mean, he sometimes asked himself, that he still felt a lingering attachment to her?

And so it was a shock to learn that Otoko had become a painter.

Oki had no idea how she might have suffered, what difficulties she might have overcome, but her accomplishment gave him keen pleasure. When he came across one of her paintings in a gallery his heart leaped. It was not her own exhibition; there was only one picture of hers—a study of a peony—among works by various artists. At the very top of the silk she had painted a single red peony. It was a full front view of the flower, larger than life, with few leaves and a single white bud low on the stem. In that unnaturally large flower he saw Otoko's pride and nobility. He bought it immediately, but since it bore her signature he decided to give it to the writers' club he belonged to, instead of taking it home. High on the club wall, the picture made a different impression on him than it had in the crowded gallery. That huge red peony looked like an apparition, loneliness seemed to radiate from deep within it. Around that time he saw a magazine photograph of Otoko in her studio.

For many years Oki had wanted to be in Kyoto for the New Year's Eve bells, but this painting had tempted him to try to hear them with Otoko.

North Kamakura was also called Yamanouchi— "Within the Hills"—and a road lined with flowering trees ran between the low hills on the north and south. Soon the blossoms along the road would signal the arrival of another spring. He had got in the habit of going out for a walk to the southern hills and it was from the crest of one of them that he gazed at the purple sunset.

The sunset lost its purple glow and became a cold, dark blue, shading off to an ashy gray. Spring seemed to have turned back to winter. The sun was gone, there was no longer any pink in the thin haze. It began to feel chilly. Oki went down into the valley and walked back to his home on one of the northern hills.

"There was a young woman here from Kyoto, a Miss Sakami," Fumiko announced. "She brought two pictures and a box of cakes."

"Is she gone already?"

"Taichiro took her to the station. Maybe they tried to find you."

"Oh?"

"She was almost frighteningly pretty," his wife said, her eyes fixed on him. "Who is she?" Oki did his best to seem unconcerned, but her feminine intuition must have told her the girl had some connection with Ueno Otoko.

"Where are the pictures?" he asked.

"In your study. They're still wrapped up, I haven't looked at them."

It seemed Keiko had done what he asked of her at Kyoto Station. Oki went to his study and unwrapped them. The two pictures were simply framed. One of them was called *Plum Tree* but showed neither branches nor trunk, only a single plum blossom as large as a baby's face. Moreover, that one blossom had both red petals and white petals. Each of the red petals was painted in an odd combination of dark and light shades of red.

The shape of this large plum blossom was not especially distorted, but it gave no impression of being a static decorative design. A strange apparition seemed to be swaying back and forth. It looked as if it were really swaying. Perhaps that was because of the background, which at first Oki had taken for thick, overlapping sheets of ice and then on closer inspection had seen as a range of snowy mountains. Only mountains would convey such a sense of vastness. But no real mountains narrowed at the base or were so jagged—that was the abstract element in her style. The background might be an image of

Keiko's own feeling. Even if you took it as cascading snowy mountains, it was not a cold snow-white. The cold of the snow and its warm color made a kind of music. The snow was not a uniform white, many colors seemed to be harmonized in it. It had the same tonality as the variations of red and white in the blossom's petals. Whether you thought of the picture as cold or warm, the plum blossom throbbed with the youthful emotions of the painter. Probably Keiko had just painted it for him, to match the season. At least, the plum blossom was recognizable.

As he looked at the painting Oki thought of the old plum tree in his garden. He had always merely accepted the gardener's opinion that it was a freak, a sport of nature, without bothering to check on the man's rather vague botanical lore. The plum tree bore red and white blossoms. Not that it had been grafted—red and white blossoms were interspersed on a single branch. Nor were all the branches like that: some had only white blossoms, some only red. However, most of the smaller branches mingled red and white together, though these were not necessarily the same branches every year. Oki loved this old plum. Just now its buds were beginning to open.

Evidently Keiko had symbolized this strange plum tree by a single blossom. No doubt she had heard about the tree from Otoko. He and Fumiko were already living in this house when he met Otoko, and, though she had never come here, he must have told her about it. She had remembered—and told her pupil.

Had she also confessed her old love?

"That's by Otoko, I suppose."

"What?" Oki turned. Absorbed by the painting, he had not noticed that his wife was standing behind him.

"Isn't that Otoko's painting?"

"Certainly not. She wouldn't do anything so youthful. It's by the girl who was just here. You see? It's signed 'Keiko.'"

"An odd picture." Fumiko's voice was hard.

"Yes, isn't it?" He made an effort to reply gently. "But young people these days, even in Japanese-style paintings . . . "

"Is this what you call abstract?"

"Well, maybe it doesn't go quite that far."

"The other one is even odder. You can't tell whether it's fish or clouds—I've never seen such a daub of colors, streaked on any old way." She knelt a little behind him, at one side.

"Hmm. Fish and clouds seem very different. Maybe it isn't either one."

"Then what is it?"

"You can take it any way you like." He bent over to glance at the back of the picture, which was leaning against the wall. "*Untitled.* She calls it *Untitled.*"

This painting had no recognizable shapes at all, and its colors were even stronger and more varied than those in *Plum Tree.* Probably because of the many horizontal lines, Fumiko had tried to see it as fish or clouds. At first glance there seemed to be no harmony among the colors, either. Yet it was unusually passionate for a picture in the classical Japanese technique. Of course there was nothing random or haphazard about it. Being untitled left it open to any interpretation, perhaps because the artist's seemingly hidden subjective feelings were in fact revealed. Oki searched for the heart of the picture.

"Just what is she to Otoko?" his wife demanded.

"A student who lives with her."

"Is that so? I want to destroy those pictures."

"Don't be ridiculous! Why are you so violent?"

"She's poured out her feelings about Otoko. They're not pictures we should keep in this house."

Startled by this lightning flash of feminine jealousy, he said quietly: "Why do you think they're about Otoko?"

"Can't you see it?"

"That's only your imagination. You're beginning to see ghosts." But as he spoke a tiny flame lighted up in his heart.

It seemed clear that the plum tree painting expressed Otoko's love for him. And so even the untitled one seemed to have the same theme. In it Keiko had also used mineral pigments, heavily overlaying them to blend with moist pigments a little below and to the left of the center of the picture. He felt he could glimpse the spirit of the picture in the strange, windowlike bright space within that overlaid portion. One could think of it as Otoko's still glowing love.

"After all, it wasn't Otoko who painted them," he said. Fumiko seemed to suspect that he had been with Otoko when he heard the temple bells in Kyoto. However, she had said nothing at the time, perhaps because it was New Year's Day.

"Anyway, I detest those pictures!" Her eyelids quivered with rage. "I won't have them in the house!"

"Whether you detest them or not, they belong to the artist. Even if she's a young girl, do you think it's right to destroy a work of art? In the first place, are you sure she's giving them to us, and not just letting us see them?"

For a moment Fumiko was silenced. Then she said: "Taichiro answered the door. Now he must have taken her to the station, though he's been gone awfully long." Was that bothering her too? The station was not far away, and trains left every fifteen minutes. "I suppose he's the one being seduced this time. A girl that pretty, with an evil fascination . . ."

Oki put the two paintings back together and began wrapping them. "Stop talking about being seduced. I don't like it. If she's all that pretty, these pictures are just herself, a young girl's narcissism."

"No, I'm certain they're about Otoko."

"Then maybe she and Otoko are lovers."

"Lovers?" Fumiko was caught off guard. "You think they're lovers?"

"I don't know. But I wouldn't be surprised if they were lesbians. Living together at an old temple in Kyoto, both of them insanely passionate, it seems."

Calling them lesbians had given Fumiko pause. When she spoke again, her voice was calm. "Even if they *are*, I think those pictures show that Otoko still loves you." Oki felt ashamed of having brought up lesbianism to talk himself out of a difficulty.

"Probably we're both wrong. We both looked at them with preconceived ideas."

"Then why did she want to paint such pictures?"

"Hmm." Realistic or not, a picture expressed the inner thoughts and feelings of the artist. But he was afraid to pursue that kind of discussion with his wife. Perhaps her first impression of Keiko's paintings had been unexpectedly accurate. And perhaps his own casual impression of lesbianism had been accurate too.

Fumiko left the study. He waited for his son to return.

Taichiro had begun to teach Japanese literature at a private college. On days when he had no lectures he would go to the departmental library at his school, or do some research at home. He had originally wanted to study "modern literature"—Japanese literature since Meiji—but because his father objected he was specializing in the Kamakura and Muromachi periods. His ability to read English, French, and German was unusual in his field. He was talented enough, but so quiet he seemed rather glum, the very opposite of his aimlessly cheerful sister Kumiko, with her smattering of flower arrangement, dressmaking, knitting, and all kinds of arts and crafts. Kumiko had always regarded her older brother as eccentric: even when she asked him to go skating or to play tennis he never gave her a decent answer. He would have nothing to do with her girl friends. He invited his students to the house, but he scarcely introduced them to her. Kumiko was not the sort to bear a grudge, but sometimes she used to pout because her mother was so solicitous toward her brother's students.

"When Taichiro has guests all we do is serve tea," her mother would respond. "But you make a great fuss, rummaging around in the refrigerator and the cupboards, or going ahead and having food brought in."

"Yes, but he has only his students!" she would reply, sniffing.

Kumiko had married and gone to London with her husband; they only heard from her two or three times a year. Taichiro was not yet financially independent and had never talked about marriage.

Oki himself began to worry at how long Taichiro had been gone.

He looked out the small French window of his study. At the base of the hill behind the house a high mound of earth, dug out during the war in making an air raid shelter, was already hidden by weeds so modest one barely noticed them. Among the weeds bloomed a mass of flowers the color of lapis lazuli. The flowers too were extremely small, but they were a bright, strong blue. Except for the sweet daphne, these flowers bloomed earlier than any in their garden. And they stayed in bloom a long time. Whatever they were, they could hardly be familiar harbingers of spring, but they were so close to his window that he often thought he would like to take one in his hand and study it. He had never yet gone to pick one, but that only seemed to increase his love for these tiny lapis-blue flowers.

Soon after them, dandelions also came to bloom in the thicket of weeds. They were long-lived too. Even now in the fading evening light you could see the yellow of dandelions and the blue of all the little flowers. For a long time Oki looked out the window.

Taichiro still had not come home.

THE FESTIVAL
OF THE
FULL MOON

Otoko was planning to take Keiko to the temple on Mt. Kurama for the Festival of the Full Moon. The festival was always held in May, but on a different date from that of the old lunar calendar. Early in the evening before the festival, the moon was rising in the clear sky over the Eastern Hills.

Otoko watched it from the veranda. "I think we'll have a fine moon tomorrow," she called in to Keiko. Visitors to the festival were supposed to drink from a sake bowl reflecting the full moon, so a cloudy, moonless night would have been disappointing.

Keiko came out on the veranda and put her hand lightly on Otoko's back.

"The moon of May," said Otoko.

Finally Keiko spoke. "Shall we go for a drive along the Eastern Hills? Or out toward Otsu, to see the moon in Lake Biwa?"

"The moon in Lake Biwa? There's nothing special about that."

"Does it look better in a sake bowl?" Keiko asked, sitting down at Otoko's feet. "Anyway, I like the colors in the garden tonight."

"Really?" Otoko looked down at the garden. "Bring a cushion, won't you? And turn off the light in there."

From the studio veranda one could see only the inner garden—the view was cut off by the temple's main residence. It was a rather artless oblong garden, but about half of it was bathed in moonlight, so that even the stepping-stones took on different colors in the light and shadow. A white azalea blooming in the shadow seemed to be floating. The scarlet maple near the veranda still had fresh young leaves, though they were darkened by the night. In spring people often mistook its bright red budding leaves for flowers, and wondered what kind of blossoms they were. The garden also had a rich cover of hair moss.

"Suppose I make some of our new tea," said Keiko. Otoko kept on gazing at her familiar garden, as if she were not used to seeing it at all hours. She was sitting there with her head slightly lowered, preoccupied, her eyes fixed on the moonlit half of the garden.

When Keiko returned with the tea she mentioned reading somewhere that Rodin's model for *The Kiss* was still alive, and around eighty years old. "It's hard to believe, isn't it?"

"That's because you're young! Must you die early if an

artist immortalized your youth? It's wrong to hunt out models like that!"

Her outburst had come from being reminded of Oki's novel. But Otoko, at thirty-nine, was beautiful. "Actually," Keiko went on calmly, "it made me think of asking you to paint me once, while I'm young."

"Of course, if I could. But why not do a self-portrait?"

"Me? I couldn't get a good likeness, for one thing. Even if I did, all sorts of ugliness would come out, and I'd end up hating the picture. And still people would think I was flattering myself, unless I made it abstract."

"You mean you'd like a realistic one? But that's out of character."

"I want *you* to paint me."

"I'd be happy to, if I could," Otoko repeated.

"Maybe your love has cooled—or are you afraid of me?" Keiko's voice had an edge to it. "A man would be delighted to paint me. Even in the nude."

Otoko seemed unperturbed. "If that's how you feel, suppose I try."

"I'm so glad!"

"But a nude won't do. A nude painted by a woman never turns out very well. Not in my old-fashioned style, anyway."

"When I paint my self-portrait I'll include you in the picture," said Keiko insinuatingly.

"What kind of picture would that be?"

Keiko giggled mysteriously. "Don't worry. If you're

going to paint me, mine can be abstract. No one will know."

"It's not that I'm worried," said Otoko, sipping the fragrant new tea.

It was the first tea of the season, a gift from the tea plantation in Uji where Otoko had been going to sketch. None of the girls picking tea appeared in her sketches: the whole surface was filled with the soft undulations of overlapping rows of tea bushes. Day after day she returned to make more sketches, in various kinds of light and shadow. Keiko always went along with her.

Once Keiko had asked: "Isn't this an abstraction?"

"If you had painted it, yes. I suppose it'll be quite daring for me, all in green, but I want to try to harmonize the colors of the young and old leaves, and the soft, rounded wave patterns."

She had made a preliminary version of the painting in her studio, on the basis of all the sketches.

But it was not merely from pleasure in the undulating waves of light and dark green that Otoko had wanted to paint the Uji tea plantation. After the breakup of her affair with Oki she had fled to Kyoto with her mother, and then gone back and forth several times to Tokyo, but what especially lingered in her mind from those days were the tea fields around Shizuoka, seen from the train window. Sometimes she saw them at midday, sometimes in the evening. She was still only a high-school student, and had no idea of becoming a painter; it was just that at the sight of the tea fields the sadness of parting sud-

denly pressed in on her. She could not say why these
rather inconspicuous green slopes had so touched her
heart, when along the railway line there were mountains,
lakes, the sea—at times even clouds dyed in sentimental
colors. But perhaps their melancholy green, and the melancholy evening shadows of the ridges across them, had
brought on the pain. Then too, they were small, well-
groomed slopes with deeply shaded ridges, not nature in
the wild; and the rows of rounded tea bushes looked like
flocks of gentle green sheep. But it may have been simply
that Otoko, sad even before leaving Tokyo, reached the
peak of her sadness the first time the train passed
Shizuoka.

When she saw the Uji tea plantation, Otoko's sadness
returned. She began going there to sketch. Even Keiko
seemed not to notice how she felt. To be sure, the spring
tea fields at Uji did not have the melancholy of those she
had seen from the train window; the green of the young
leaves was too bright.

Although Keiko had read Oki's novel, and had heard
all about him during their long talks in bed together, she
still seemed unaware that the sketches of the tea plantation harbored the sadness of Otoko's old love. She herself delighted in the pattern of softly rounded overlapping rows of tea bushes, but the more sketches she
turned out the further they were from reality. Otoko
found these rough sketches amusing.

"You're going to do the whole picture in green, aren't
you?" said Keiko.

"Of course. The tea fields at picking time—variations in green, you know."

"I'm trying to make up my mind whether to use red, or purple, or what. I don't care if people can't tell it's a tea field."

Keiko's preliminary study was propped up against the studio wall alongside Otoko's.

"Such delicious new tea," said Otoko, smiling. "Do make some more—in the abstract style."

"So bitter you can't drink it?"

"Is that what you call abstract?" She heard Keiko's young laughter from the other room. Her voice hardened slightly. "When you went to Tokyo you stopped in at Kamakura, didn't you?"

"Yes."

"Why?"

"On New Year's Day Mr. Oki asked to see my paintings." She paused, then went on coldly, "Otoko, I want to get revenge for you."

"Revenge?" Otoko was shocked. "Revenge for me?"

"That's right."

"Keiko, come sit here. Let's talk about it over some of your abstract tea."

Silently Keiko knelt at her side, her knees grazing Otoko's, and picked up a cup of green tea. "My, it *is* bitter!" she said, frowning. "Let me make a new pot."

"Never mind," said Otoko, restraining her. "Why on earth are you talking about revenge?"

"You know why."

"I've never thought of such a thing. I have no wish for it."

"Because you still love him—because you can't stop loving him, as long as you live." Keiko's voice choked. "So I want revenge."

"But why?"

"I have my own jealousy!"

"Really?" Otoko put her hand on Keiko's shoulder; it was trembling.

"It's true, isn't it? I can tell. I hate it."

"Such a violent child," said Otoko softly. "What can you mean by revenge? What are you planning to do?"

Keiko was looking down, motionless. The band of moonlight in the garden had broadened.

"Why did you go to Kamakura, without even telling me?"

"I wanted to see the family of the man who made you so unhappy."

"And did you?"

"Only his son Taichiro—I suppose he's the image of his father when *he* was young. It seems he studies medieval Japanese literature. Anyway, he was very kind to me, he showed me around the Kamakura temples and even took me down the coast, to Enoshima."

"But you're a Tokyoite, surely those places weren't new to you?"

"Yes, but I never saw much of them before. Enoshima has changed enormously. And I enjoyed hearing about the temple where women could escape their husbands."

"Is that your revenge, seducing that boy? Or being

seduced by him?" Otoko let her hand drop from Keiko's shoulder. "It looks as if I'm the one who ought to be jealous."

"Oh, Otoko, *you* jealous? That makes me happy!" She put her arms around Otoko's neck and leaned against her. "You see? To anyone but you I could be wicked, a real devil!"

"But you took two of your favorite pictures."

"Even a wicked girl wants to make a good impression. Taichiro wrote to say my paintings are hanging in his study."

"Is that your revenge for me?" said Otoko quietly. "The beginning of your revenge?"

"Yes."

"He was only an infant, he didn't know anything about me and his father. What hurt me was later, hearing about the birth of his little sister. Now that I look back on it, I'm sure that's how I felt. I suppose she's married by now."

"Shall I break up her marriage?"

"Really, Keiko! You're much too vain, even joking like that. You'll get into trouble. It's not just a piece of harmless mischief."

"As long as I have you I'm not afraid. How do you suppose I'd paint if I lost you? Maybe I'd give up my painting—and my life."

"Don't say such an awful thing!"

"I wonder if you couldn't have broken up Mr. Oki's marriage."

"But I was only a schoolgirl . . . and they had a child."

"I'd have done it."

"You don't know how strong a family can be."

"Stronger than art?"

"Well . . . " Otoko tilted her head, looking a little sad. "In those days I didn't think about art."

"Otoko." Keiko turned to her, holding her gently by the wrist. "Why did you have me go to meet Mr. Oki, and see him off?"

"Because you're young and pretty, of course! Because I'm proud of you."

"I hate your hiding things from me. And I was watching you carefully—with my jealous eyes."

"Were you?" Otoko looked into Keiko's eyes, sparkling in the moonlight. "It's not that I wanted to hide anything from you. But I was only sixteen when we were separated, and now I'm middle-aged, beginning to thicken around the waist. The truth is, I didn't feel much like meeting him. I was afraid he'd be disillusioned."

"Shouldn't he have been the one to worry? I admire you more than anyone I've ever known, so I was disillusioned by him. Since coming to live with you I find young men a bore, but I thought Mr. Oki would be more impressive. As soon as I saw him I was utterly disillusioned. Your memories gave me the impression of a much finer person."

"You can't tell on such short acquaintance."

"I certainly can."

"How can you?"

"I'd have no trouble seducing Mr. Oki *or* his son."

"You frighten me!" exclaimed Otoko, blanching.

"Keiko, that kind of conceitedness is dangerous."

"Not in the least," said Keiko, quite unperturbed.

"It *is*," Otoko insisted. "And aren't you being terribly predatory? No matter how young and beautiful you are."

"I suppose most women are what you call predatory."

"Indeed. And is that why you took your favorite pictures to Mr. Oki?"

"No. I don't need pictures to seduce him."

Otoko seemed appalled.

"It's just that I'm your pupil, so I wanted him to see my best work."

"I'm grateful. But you say you only exchanged a few words with him at the station. Was that any reason to give away your pictures?"

"I promised. Besides, I wondered how he would react to them, and I needed a pretext for going to meet his family."

"It's a good thing he was out!"

"I imagine he saw the pictures later, but he probably didn't understand them."

"You're being unfair to him."

"Even in his novels he never wrote anything better than *A Girl of Sixteen*."

"That's not true. You're fond of it because he idealized me in it. A youthful novel like that appeals to young people. I can see why you wouldn't care for his later works."

"Anyway, if he died today it's the only novel he'd be remembered for."

"Stop talking like that!" Otoko's voice was stern. She

drew her wrist out of Keiko's grasp and edged away.

"Are you still so attached to him?" Keiko's voice was also harsh. "Even though I said I'd get revenge for you?"

"It's not attachment."

"Is it . . . love?"

"Perhaps."

Abruptly Otoko got up and went inside. Keiko stayed out on the moonlit veranda, sitting with her face buried in her hands.

"Otoko, I'm living for someone else too!" Her voice trembled. "But when it's a man like Mr. Oki . . . "

"Forgive me. It all happened when I was so young."

"I'm going to get revenge."

"That wouldn't destroy my love."

Keiko was weeping on the veranda, still with her face in her hands. "Paint me, Otoko . . . before I turn into the kind of woman you said. Please! Let me pose in the nude for you."

"All right. I'd love doing a portrait of you."

"I'm glad!"

Otoko had stored away a number of sketches of her dead baby. Years had passed, but she still intended to use them for a painting to be called *The Ascension of an Infant.* She had searched through albums of Western art for pictures of cherubs and of the Christ child, but their plump good health seemed inappropriate to her sorrow. There were several famous old Japanese paintings of Saint Kobo as a boy that touched her with their typically graceful expression of restrained emotion. Yet the saint was neither an infant nor was he ascending to heaven.

Not that Otoko wanted to show the ascension as such, only to suggest that kind of spiritual feeling. But would she ever finish it?

Now that Keiko had asked to be painted, Otoko thought of her old sketches for *The Ascension of an Infant.* Perhaps she could portray Keiko in the manner of the paintings of the boy saint. It would be a purely classical *Portrait of a Holy Virgin.* Though works of religious art, some of the saint's portraits had an indescribably seductive charm.

"Keiko, I do want to paint you," said Otoko, "and I've just thought of a design. It'll be in the Buddhist tradition, so I can't have any sort of improper pose."

"Buddhist?" Keiko shifted uneasily. "I'm not sure I care for the idea."

"Well, let me try. Buddhist paintings are often very beautiful—and I could call it *A Girl Abstractionist.*"

"You're teasing me."

"I'm serious. I'll do it as soon as I've finished the tea plantation." Otoko looked back at the studio wall. Over their pictures of the tea plantation hung her portrait of her mother.

Otoko let her eyes rest on the portrait.

Her mother looked young and beautiful in it, even younger than herself. Perhaps that reflected Otoko's own age of thirty-one or -two at the time she painted it. Or perhaps it had just turned out that way.

When Keiko first saw it she had said: "Lovely. This looks like a self-portrait." Does it really? Otoko had wondered.

Otoko resembled her mother. Was it out of longing for her dead mother that so much of the resemblance was captured in this portrait? At first she had made a great many sketches based on a photograph, but none of these had moved her. Then she decided to ignore the photograph—and there was her mother sitting before her. Rather than a phantom, it was her living image. Over and over she made new sketches, swiftly, her heart overflowing with emotion. But frequently she paused, eyes clouded with tears. She realized that the portrait of her mother was becoming more like a self-portrait.

The final result was the picture now hanging on the wall over the studies of the tea plantation. Otoko had burned all the earlier versions. The remaining one looked most like a self-portrait, but Otoko thought it would do. Whenever she looked at it, there was a hint of sadness in her eyes. The picture breathed with her. How long had it taken her to fix the image into this portrait?

Until now Otoko had painted no other portraits, and only a few small figure paintings of any kind. Yet tonight, pressed by Keiko, she suddenly felt like doing a portrait. Otoko had never thought of her *Ascension of an Infant* in that way. But that long-cherished wish must explain why she was reminded of the portraits of the boy saint, and wanted to paint Keiko in classical Buddhist style. Her mother, her lost baby, and Keiko—were they not her three loves? Different as they were, she should paint all three of them.

"Otoko," Keiko called. "You're looking at your mother's picture, and wondering how you can paint me, aren't you? You think you can't possibly have that kind of love for me." She came in and sat close beside her.

"Silly! I'm dissatisfied now when I look at it—I've improved a little since then, you know. Anyway, I'm still fond of the picture. For all its faults, it's one I devoted myself to heart and soul."

"You needn't go to such pains over *my* picture. Just dash it off."

"No, no," said Otoko, her thoughts elsewhere. Looking at the portrait had brought a flood of memories of her mother. Then Keiko had called to her, and Otoko was reminded once again of the old portraits of the boy saint. Some of the figures looked like pretty little girls or beautiful young maidens, in the elegant, refined manner of Buddhist art but also with a certain voluptuousness. They could be taken as symbols of the homosexual love at medieval monasteries where women were forbidden, of the yearning for handsome boys who could be mistaken for beautiful young girls. Perhaps that was why the saint's portraits had come to mind as soon as she thought of painting Keiko. The hair style was not unlike the bobbed hair and bangs worn by little girls today. However, one no longer saw such resplendent brocade kimonos except in the No theater; they would seem much too old-fashioned for a modern young woman. Otoko recalled Kishida Ryusei's portraits of his daughter Reiko. They were oils or water colors minutely drawn in a meticulous classical style influenced by Dürer: some of them were like religious paintings. But Otoko had seen an extremely rare one, in light colors on Chinese paper, that showed Reiko in a red underskirt naked above the waist. She was sitting in a formal pose. It was hardly one of Ryusei's masterpieces, and Otoko wondered why he had portrayed his own daughter that way, in a painting in classical Japanese style. He had done similar things in Western style.

Why not paint a nude of Keiko, then? She could still follow the design of the boy saint's portrait, and there were even Buddhist figures that gave the hint of a woman's breasts. But what of the hair style? She had seen a superb portrait by Kobayashi Kokei, of exquisite purity, but that too had the wrong sort of coiffure. Pondering various solutions, Otoko felt all the more keenly that it was beyond her powers.

"Keiko, shall we go to bed?" she asked.

"So early? With such a lovely moon?" Keiko turned to look at the clock. "It's only five minutes of ten."

"I'm a little tired. Can't we talk lying down?"

"All right."

While Otoko was at the dressing table Keiko prepared their beds. She was very quick at it. After Otoko got up, Keiko went to the mirror to remove her makeup. Leaning over, curving her slender neck, she stared at the face in the mirror.

"Otoko, I'm not the right person for a Buddhist painting."

"That depends on the artist."

Keiko took out her hairpins and shook her head.

"Are you undoing your hair?"

"Yes." As Keiko combed the long strands, Otoko watched from her bed.

"You're taking down your hair tonight?"

"I think it's getting an odor. I should have washed it." Keiko sniffed at a handful of her back hair. "Otoko, how old were you when your father died?"

"Eleven, of course! How many times are you going to ask me?"

Keiko said nothing. She closed the paper-screened doors to the veranda, and the doors between the bedroom and the studio, and lay down beside Otoko. The two beds were together.

For several nights they had gone to bed without closing the outside shutters. The paper screens facing the garden glowed faintly in the moonlight.

Otoko's mother had died of lung cancer, without revealing to her that Otoko had a younger half-sister by a different mother. Otoko had never been told.

Her father had been in the export-import trade in silk and wool. A great many people attended his funeral, bowing and offering incense in the usual fashion, but Otoko's mother noticed among the mourners a rather strange young woman who seemed to be of mixed blood. When she bowed to the bereaved family, her eyes looked swollen from weeping. Otoko's mother felt a sharp pang. She nodded to summon her husband's private secretary, and whispered to him to inquire at the reception desk

about the Eurasian-looking young woman. Later the
secretary was able to learn that her grandmother was a
Canadian who had married a Japanese man, and she
herself had gone to a school for Americans and was
working as an interpreter. He said she lived in a small
house in Azabu.

"I suppose she has no children."

"They say there's a little girl."

"Did you see her?"

"No, I heard it from people in the neighborhood."

She felt sure that the little girl was her husband's child.
There were ways to verify it, but she thought the young
woman herself might come to see her. She never came.
Over half a year later Otoko's mother was told by the
secretary that she had married, taking the child along to
her new home. He also intimated that the Eurasian
woman had been her husband's mistress. As time passed,
her jealous indignation cooled. She began to wish she
could adopt the little girl. Her own husband's child must
be growing up unaware of her real father. She felt as if
she had lost something precious—and not merely because Otoko was her only child. Yet she could not tell an
eleven-year-old girl about her father's illegitimate
daughter. By now her sister would have been married for
some years, in the normal course of events, and perhaps
also have children of her own. But for Otoko it was as if
she did not exist. . . .

"Otoko, Otoko!" Keiko was sitting up in bed, shaking

her. "Did you have a nightmare? You seemed to be in pain." As Otoko gasped for breath, Keiko leaned over her and stroked her chest.

"Were you watching me?"

"Yes, for a while."

"How mean of you! I was having a dream."

"What kind of dream?"

"About a green person." Otoko's voice was still agitated.

"Somebody dressed in green?"

"Not the clothing. It was green all over, including the arms and legs."

"The green-eyed monster?"

"Don't make fun of me! It wasn't fierce-looking, just a green figure floating lightly round and round my bed."

"A woman?"

Otoko did not reply.

"It's a good dream. I'm sure it is!" Keiko put her hand over Otoko's eyes and pressed them shut; then she took up one of Otoko's fingers in her other hand, and bit it.

"Ouch!" Otoko opened her eyes wide.

Keiko interpreted the dream for her. "You said you'd paint me, remember. So I've taken on the green of the tea plantation."

"Do you think so? You're dancing all around me even when you're asleep? That frightens me!"

Keiko let her head drop on Otoko's breast, and tittered a little hysterically. "But it's *your* dream. . . . "

The following day they climbed up to the temple on Mt. Kurama, arriving toward evening. Worshipers were gathered in the temple compound. The late dusk of a long May day had already settled on the surrounding peaks and tall forests.

Over the Eastern Hills beyond Kyoto the full moon had risen. Watch fires were burning on the left and right before the main hall of the temple. The priests had come out and begun to chant the sutras, repeating the sacred words in chorus after the scarlet-robed head priest. A harmonium accompanied them.

All the worshipers offered lighted candles. Directly in front of the main hall was a huge silver sake bowl filled with water, reflecting the full moon. Water from the bowl was poured into the cupped hands of each of the worshipers; one by one they came forward, bowed, and drank it. Otoko and Keiko did the same.

"When we get home you may find green footprints in your room!" said Keiko. She seemed exhilarated by the atmosphere of the mountain ceremony.

A RAINY SKY

When Oki was tired of writing, or when a novel was going badly, he would lie down on the couch in the open corridor beside his study. In the afternoon he would often fall asleep there for an hour or two. Only in the past few years had he got into the habit of taking such naps. He used to go out for a walk instead, but after so many years in Kamakura he had become all too familiar with the nearby temples, and even with the hills. Then too, being an early riser, he always took a short walk in the morning. Once awake, he could not bear to loll about in bed; also, he preferred to be out of the way while the maid tidied up the house. Before dinner he took a fairly long walk.

The corridor beside his study was a wide one, with a writing table and chair in the corner. He wrote either there or at a low table on the matted floor of the study.

The couch in the corridor was very comfortable. When he stretched out on it his difficulties vanished from his mind. It was uncanny. While he was writing a novel he tended to sleep poorly at night and to dream about his work, but on the couch in the corridor he quickly fell into a deep sleep that blotted out everything. When he was young he never had a nap. Often the whole afternoon would be taken up by callers. He wrote at night, usually from midnight till dawn. Now that he worked during the day he had begun taking naps, but not at any fixed time. Whenever he felt blocked in his writing he lay down on the couch. Sometimes it was in the morning, sometimes almost evening. Only rarely did he feel, as he used to when he worked at night, that fatigue stimulated his imagination.

My naps must be a sign of age, Oki thought. But the couch was magical.

Whenever he rested on it he fell asleep and awakened refreshed. Not infrequently he could find a new pathway through the difficulties that had brought his writing to a standstill. A magic couch.

Now they were in the rainy season—the season he disliked most. Their house was some distance from the ocean and separated from it by hills, but extremely damp. The sky hung low. Oki felt a dull blurring and heaviness over his right temple, as if mold were growing on the folds of his brain. There were days when he slept twice, morning and afternoon, on the magic couch.

One afternoon the maid announced that someone

from Kyoto called Sakami had come to see him. Oki had just awakened but was still lying on the couch. "Shall I say you're resting?" she asked.

"No. It's a young lady?"

"Yes, sir. She was here once before."

"Show her into the parlor, please."

He let his head sink back again and closed his eyes. The nap had lightened his rainy season dullness but the thought of Keiko was even more refreshing. He rose and washed and went out to the parlor. As soon as she saw him, Keiko got up from her chair. She was blushing slightly.

"I'm sorry to drop in on you like this."

"It's good of you to come. I was out for a walk the other time and just missed you. You should have stayed a little longer."

"Taichiro saw me to the station."

"So I hear. I believe he showed you around Kamakura."

"Yes."

"Since you're from Tokyo, that must have been nothing new. And of course it doesn't compare with Kyoto or Nara."

Keiko looked straight into his eyes. "There was a beautiful sunset over the ocean."

Oki was surprised to learn that his son had gone all the way to the shore with her. "I haven't seen you since New Year's Day," he remarked. "Half a year has gone by already."

"Mr. Oki, is that a long time? Does half a year seem long to you?"

He wondered what she was getting at. "I suppose it depends on how you think of it," he said. Keiko was unsmiling, as if disdainful of his reply. "If you couldn't meet a lover for half a year, wouldn't it seem like a long time?"

Keiko remained silent, with the same disdainful expression. Her greenish eyes seemed to challenge him. Oki became a little annoyed. "After half a year of pregnancy you can feel the baby move in your womb," he went on, trying to embarrass her. She did not respond. "Anyway, we've come from winter to summer, though it's still this miserable rainy season. . . . Even philosophers don't seem to have any satisfactory explanation of time. People say time will solve everything, but I have my doubts about that, too. What do you think, Miss Sakami? Is death the end of it all?"

"I'm not such a pessimist."

"I wouldn't call it pessimism," said Oki, to be contradictory. "Of course the same half year for me and for a young woman like you would be very different. Or suppose someone had cancer with only half a year to live. Then again, some people have their lives cut off suddenly in a traffic accident, or in war. Some are murdered."

"But you *are* an artist, Mr. Oki, aren't you?"

"I'm afraid I'll leave behind only things I'm ashamed of."

"You needn't be ashamed of any of your works."

"I wish that were true. But maybe everything I've done will disappear. I'd like that."

"How can you say such a thing? You must realize your novel about my teacher is going to last."

"That novel again!" Oki frowned. "Even you bring it up, knowing her as you do."

"It's because I do know her. I can't help it."

"Well, perhaps not."

Her expression livened. "Mr. Oki, did you ever fall in love again?"

"Yes, I suppose so. But not the way it was with Otoko."

"Why haven't you written about it?"

"Well . . . " He hesitated. "She made it clear she didn't want me to put her in a book."

"Really?"

"Maybe it indicates a kind of weakness on my part, as a writer. But I don't imagine I could have poured out that much emotion a second time."

"I wouldn't care what you wrote about me."

"Oh?" This was only his third meeting with her—indeed, you could hardly call them "meetings." How could he possibly write about her, except to borrow her beauty for one of his characters? She did say she went down to the shore with his son. Had anything happened then?

"So I've found a good model," said Oki, laughing to hide his suspicions. But as he looked at her, the strange, seductive charm of her eyes stilled his laughter. Her eyes were so moist that she almost seemed to be in tears.

"Miss Ueno has promised to do a portrait of me," Keiko said.

"Has she?"

"And I brought another picture to show you."

"I can't say I know much about abstract paintings, but I'd like to see it. Let's look at it in the next room, where it's not so cramped. My son has the two you brought last time hanging in his study."

"He isn't home today?"

"No, this is one of his days at the university. My wife went to the theater."

"I'm glad you're alone," Keiko murmured, and went to the entryway to get her painting. She brought it in to the Japanese-style sitting room. The picture was in a simple frame of unpainted wood. Its dominant tone was green, but she had boldly dashed on a variety of colors to suit her whim. The whole surface was seething and undulating.

"Mr. Oki, this is realistic for me. It's a tea field at Uji."

He crouched to peer at it. "It's a tea field that looks like surging waves—a tea field swelling with youth. At first I wondered if it symbolized a heart bursting into flames."

"That makes me so happy! To have you see it that way . . . " Keiko knelt behind him, her chin almost on his shoulder, as he studied the picture. Her sweet breath warmed his hair. "I'm so happy," she repeated. "Happy you could see my heart in it! Though it's not much as a picture of a tea field."

"It's really youthful."

"Of course I went out to the tea field to sketch, but it

was only for the first hour or so that I saw it as rows of tea bushes."

"Oh?"

"The plantation was very quiet. Then all those rounded, rolling waves of fresh green began to stir, and finally it came out like this. It's not abstract."

"But I should think a tea field would seem rather subdued, even when the new growth is sprouting."

"I never have learned how to be subdued! Not in art, nor in my emotions."

"Not even in your emotions?" As he turned toward her his shoulder touched the softness of her breast. His eyes stopped before one of her ears. "If you keep on at that rate, you may find yourself cutting off one of those pretty ears."

"I'm not a genius like Van Gogh! Someone will have to bite it off for me."

Startled, Oki twisted sharply around to her, and Keiko caught hold of him to steady herself.

"I detest subdued emotions," she said, not shifting her position. With the least pressure she would have collapsed helplessly into his arms, ready to be kissed.

But he did not move. She remained motionless too.

"Mr. Oki," she whispered, her gaze fixed on him.

"Your ears are lovely," he said, "but there's a kind of eerie beauty to your profile."

"I'm glad you think so!" Her slender neck flushed slightly. "I'll never forget that, as long as I live. But how long will beauty last? A woman feels sad to think of that."

He had no reply.

"It's embarrassing to be stared at, but any woman would be delighted to seem beautiful to a man like you."

Oki was astonished at the warmth of her response. She might have been uttering words of love. "I'm delighted too," he said gravely. "Though you must be beautiful in many ways I've never seen."

"Do you think so? I don't know, I'm not a model, just someone who's trying to paint."

"A painter has a right to use a model. Sometimes I envy that."

"If I'm any good to you . . . "

"That's very kind."

"I said I wouldn't care what you wrote about me. I'm sorry I can't equal the girl of your imagination, that's all."

"Should I be realistic?"

"Whatever you please."

"An artist's model and a writer's model are entirely different, you know."

"Of course." Keiko blinked her rich eyelashes. "But my tea-field sketch isn't just a scene from nature. It's turned out to be about myself."

"All pictures are like that, aren't they? Even abstractions. But a model has to be another live human being. Novels need human beings too, no matter how much you write about landscapes."

"Mr. Oki, I'm a human being!"

"A beautiful one," he said, helping her up. "But even a nude artist's model only has to pose. That's not quite enough for a novelist."

"I know."

"Do you?"

"Yes."

Oki found the girl's boldness inhibiting. "I suppose I could borrow your looks for a character in a novel."

"That doesn't sound like much fun." She seemed deliberately coquettish.

"Women are odd," he said, to extricate himself. "Two or three of them have told me they're sure I modeled one of my characters on them. And they were complete strangers, women I'd had nothing to do with. What kind of delusion could that be?"

"Lots of women are unhappy, so they console themselves with delusions."

"Isn't there something wrong with them?"

"It's easy for a woman to go wrong. You can make a woman go wrong, can't you?"

Her question left him at a loss. "Do you just coldly wait for it to happen?"

He tried to change the drift of the conversation. "Anyway, being a novelist's model is different. It's an unrewarded sacrifice."

"I love to sacrifice myself! Maybe that's my reason for living." Again she had astonished him.

"In your case it's willful, as if you're demanding the other person's sacrifice."

"That's not true. Sacrifice comes from love. It's from yearning."

"Are you sacrificing yourself to Otoko?"

She did not answer.

"That's right, isn't it?"

"Maybe I was, but Otoko is a woman, after all. There's nothing pure about one woman devoting her life to another."

"That's something I wouldn't know."

"Both of them may be destroyed."

"Destroyed?"

"Yes." After a moment she went on: "I hate to have the slightest doubt. I don't care if it only lasts five or ten days, I want someone who can make me forget myself completely."

"That's asking a lot, even of marriage, isn't it?"

"I've had marriage offers, but that kind of devotion doesn't count. I don't want to be concerned about myself. As I said, I detest subdued emotions."

"You seem to feel you ought to commit suicide a few days after you fall in love with someone."

"I'm not afraid of suicide. The worst thing is being sick of life. I'd be happy if you strangled me—after you used me as a model, that is."

Oki tried to dispel the feeling that Keiko had come to seduce him; perhaps she was not such a designing woman. In any event, she might be quite an interesting model for a character. Yet it did not seem unlikely that a love affair followed by a separation would drive her, as it had Otoko, into a psychiatric ward.

Early this spring when Keiko had brought her other two pictures Taichiro had received her, and then left the house to go out with her all the way to the ocean beyond Kamakura. Obviously she had captivated his son.

But she'd ruin him, Oki thought. He told himself he was not merely being jealous.

"I hope you'll hang this one in your study," Keiko said.

"Suppose I do," he replied half-heartedly.

"I want you to catch a glimpse of it in a dimly lit room at night. Then the green of the tea fields will sink into the background, and all my gaudy colors will come floating out."

"I imagine it would give me queer dreams."

"What kind of dreams, I wonder?"

"Well—young dreams, no doubt."

"How nice of you to say so! Do you really mean it?"

"You're young, after all," said Oki. "Those rounded waves of tea bushes reflect Otoko's influence, but the colors seem to be you yourself."

"One day will be enough, I don't care if it gathers dust in your closet after that. It's a bad picture. Before long I'm going to come and slash it to ribbons!"

"What!"

"I mean it," she said, looking curiously gentle. "It's a bad picture. But if you'll just hang it in your study for a day . . . "

He did not know what to reply. Keiko hung her head. "I wonder if this funny picture really will bring you any dreams."

"I'm afraid I'll be tempted to dream about you."

"Please do, dream whatever you like." An unexpected flush tinged her beautiful ears. "But Mr. Oki," she said, looking up at him, "you haven't done anything to make yourself dream about me." Her eyes clouded slightly.

"Let me see you off, then, the way my son did. There's no one at home, so I can't offer you dinner. I'll call a taxi."

Their taxi passed Kamakura and went along the Shichiri Beach. Keiko was silent.

Both the sea and the sky were gray.

Oki had the taxi stop at the Enoshima Marineland across from the island.

He bought cuttlefish and mackerel to feed the dolphins. The dolphins leaped from the water to take the bait out of Keiko's hand. She became more daring and held the bait higher and higher. The dolphins kept jumping higher after it. Keiko was as delighted as a child. She did not even notice that it was beginning to rain.

"Let's leave before it gets any heavier," he urged her. "Your clothes must already be damp."

"That was fun!"

In the car Oki remarked that schools of dolphins sometimes came in on the other side of the bay, a little beyond Ito. "They get chased close to shore, and then men strip down and catch them in their bare arms. Dolphins can't resist if you tickle them under their fins."

"Poor things."

"I wonder if a nice young girl could resist it."

"What a repulsive thought! I suppose she'd scratch and claw and lash out."

"Probably the dolphins would be gentler."

The taxi arrived at a hotel on a hilltop overlooking Enoshima. The island was gray too, and the Miura Peninsula stretched out vaguely to the left. Rain was coming down in large drops, and the usual thick haze of the season hung in the air. Even the nearby pines were misty.

By the time they were shown to a room they felt thoroughly wet and sticky.

"We can't go back," Oki said. "The fog is too thick."

Keiko nodded. He was surprised at how readily she agreed.

"We ought to have a bath before dinner." He rubbed his hand over his face. "Shall we play dolphin?"

"You do say repulsive things—mentioning me in the same breath with a fish! Must you be so insulting? Playing dolphin!" She leaned against the frame of the window. "It's a dark ocean."

"I'm sorry."

"You might say you'd like to see me naked. Or just take me in your arms."

"You wouldn't resist?"

"I don't know—but asking me to play dolphin is an insult! I'm no slut, after all. You seem so depraved."

"Do I?" he said, and went into the bathroom.

Oki took a shower, gave the tub a quick rinse, and began filling it. When he came out his hair was disheveled and he was rubbing his body with a towel. "I'm drawing a hot bath for you," he said, not looking at her. "It must be half full by now."

Keiko was gazing out at the ocean, her face set. "It's turned into a heavy drizzle. You can barely see the island or the peninsula."

"Are you sad?"

"I hate the color of those waves, too."

"You must feel sticky all over. Go and have your bath, why don't you?"

She nodded, and went into the bathroom. There was no sound of splashing. But she came back looking freshly bathed, and sat down at the vanity table and opened her handbag.

Oki went over behind her. "I washed my hair in the shower, but all they had was pomade, and I don't care for the smell of it."

"Try some of my perfume." Keiko handed him a small vial.

Oki sniffed at it. "Am I supposed to sprinkle this over the pomade?"

"Only a tiny bit!" she said, smiling.

He grasped her hand. "Keiko, don't put any makeup on."

"You're hurting me!" She turned toward him. "Naughty, aren't you?"

"I like you just as you are. Such beautiful teeth, and eyebrows." He pressed his lips to her glowing cheek. She gave a little cry as her chair tilted over, and she fell with it. Now Oki's lips were on hers.

It was a long kiss.

He drew his head back to take a breath.

"No, no, don't stop!" Keiko held him closer.

Concealing his surprise, he tried to make a joke of it. "Even pearl divers can't stay under water that long. You'll faint."

"Make me. . . . "

"Of course women have more stamina——" Again he

kissed her for a long time. Short of breath once more, he took her up in his arms and laid her on the bed. She curled herself into a ball.

Although she did not resist, he had difficulty uncurling her. Meanwhile it became obvious that she was not a virgin. He began to handle her more roughly.

Just then Keiko cried out plaintively from beneath him: "Oh! . . . Otoko, Otoko!"

"What?"

Oki had thought she was calling out to him, but his strength ebbed when he realized she was actually calling Otoko. "What did you say? Otoko?" His voice was sober. Keiko pushed him away without answering.

A STONE
GARDEN

Among the many famous old stone gardens in Kyoto are those of the Moss Temple, the Silver Pavilion, and Ryoanji; indeed, the latter is almost too famous, though it may be said to embody the very essence of Zen aesthetics. Otoko knew them all and had images of them in her mind. But since the end of the rainy season she had been going to the Moss Temple to sketch its stone garden. Not that she thought she could paint it. She only wanted to absorb a little of its strength.

Was this not one of the oldest and most powerful of all stone gardens? Otoko had no real desire to make a painting of it. The stone landscape on the hillside had none of the gentle beauty of the so-called moss garden below. Except for the sightseers passing by, she would have liked just to gaze on and on at it. Perhaps she sketched to avoid arousing the curiosity of the people who saw her stand looking at it from one angle and then another.

The Moss Temple was restored in 1339 by the priest Muso, who refurbished the temple buildings and had a pond dug and an island constructed. It is said that he would lead visitors up to a look-out pavilion at the top of the hill to enjoy the view of Kyoto. All those buildings had been destroyed. The garden must have been restored many times, after floods and other calamities. Apparently the present dry landscape symbolizing a waterfall and a stream was constructed along a path lighted by stone lanterns leading up to the look-out pavilion. Since it was a stone arrangement, it had probably remained unchanged.

Otoko came here only to sketch and to look at the stone garden, and had no interest in its historical associations. Keiko followed her like a shadow.

"All stone compositions are abstract, aren't they?" Keiko remarked one day. "There's something of that strength in Cézanne's painting of the rocky coasts at L'Estaque."

"You've seen that? Of course it was an actual landscape—not huge cliffs, perhaps, but massive outcroppings along the shore."

"Otoko, if you paint this stone garden it'll turn out to be abstract. I couldn't even attempt it realistically."

"I suppose you're right. Though I'm not suggesting I'll paint it."

"Shall I try a rough sketch?"

"That might be best. I liked your picture of the tea plantation—it seemed so young. You took that one to Mr. Oki's house too, didn't you?"

"Yes. By now his wife may have ripped it to shreds. . . . I spent the night with him at a hotel near Enoshima. He seemed awfully depraved, but when I called your name it quieted him down immediately. He still loves you, and he has a guilty conscience. It's enough to make me jealous."

"But what on earth were you up to?"

"I want to break up his family, to get revenge for you."

"Revenge again!"

"I hate it. You're still in love with him, in spite of everything. Women are such fools—that's what I hate!" She paused. "It's why I'm jealous."

"Are you?"

"Of course."

"You spent the night with him out of jealousy? If I still love him, shouldn't *I* be jealous?"

"But are you?"

Otoko made no reply.

"I'd be so happy if you were!" Keiko began sketching swiftly. "I couldn't get to sleep at the hotel, though Mr. Oki seemed to fall asleep quite contentedly. I can't stand men in their fifties."

Otoko found herself wondering if they had had a double bed.

"He was sound asleep. It was a marvelous feeling, to know I could strangle him there."

"You *are* dangerous."

"It was just a feeling. But it made me so happy I couldn't sleep."

"And you say it's all for my sake?" Otoko's hand trembled as she went on sketching. "I can't believe it."

"Certainly it's for you!"

Otoko was beginning to feel even more alarmed. "Please don't go to that house again. There's no telling what might happen."

"Didn't you ever want to kill him yourself, when you were in the hospital?"

"Never. I may have been out of my mind, but as for killing anyone . . . "

"You didn't hate him, you were too much in love with him?"

"Then there was my baby."

"The baby?" Keiko hesitated. "Maybe I could have one by him."

"Keiko!"

"And then ruin him."

Otoko stared at her. Frightening words were coming from that beautiful throat. "I suppose you could," she said, controlling herself. "But do you understand what that means? If you had his child I couldn't look after you. And once you had a baby you wouldn't talk like that. Everything would change for you."

"I'll never change!"

What had actually happened at the hotel with Oki? Otoko suspected that she was hiding something. What was Keiko trying to conceal behind such violent words as jealousy and revenge?

Otoko asked herself if she could still be jealous over Oki, and shut her eyelids. The stone garden lingered like a shadow in the depths of her eyes.

"Otoko! Are you all right?" Keiko hugged her. "You're looking so pale!" Then she pinched her hard under the arms.

"That hurts!" Otoko reeled, and Keiko steadied her.

"Otoko, you're all I want. Only you."

In silence Otoko wiped the cold perspiration from her forehead. "If you go on like that you'll end up unhappy for the rest of your life."

"I'm not afraid of unhappiness."

"You're young and pretty, so you can say that."

"As long as I can be with you I'll be happy."

"I'm glad—but after all, I'm a woman."

"I hate men."

"That won't do," said Otoko sadly. "If that's true, the longer we're together . . . Besides, our tastes in art are completely different."

"I'd hate to have a teacher who painted the same way I did."

"You have lots of hates, haven't you?" said Otoko, somewhat more calmly. "Let me see your sketchbook a moment."

Keiko handed it over.

"And what is this?"

"Don't be mean! The stone garden, of course. Look

closely. I've done something I thought I couldn't."

As Otoko studied it, her expression changed. A rough ink sketch was hard to interpret, but it seemed to vibrate with a mysterious life. The sketch had a quality hitherto lacking in Keiko's work. "So there *was* something between you and Mr. Oki at the hotel."

"I wouldn't say so."

"Your sketch is like nothing you've ever done before!"

"Otoko, to tell the truth, he can't even manage a long kiss."

Otoko was silent.

"Are all men like that? . . . It was my first time with a man, you know."

Disturbed by the implications of that "first time," Otoko went on looking at Keiko's sketch. "I wish I were a stone myself," she said at last.

The priest Muso's stone garden, weathered for centuries, had taken on such an antique patina that the stones looked as if they had always been there. However, their stiff, angular forms left no doubt that it was a human composition, and Otoko had never felt its pressure as intensely as she did now. She felt as if she were under a crushing spiritual weight. "Shall we go home?" she asked. "The stones are beginning to frighten me."

"All right."

"I can't just sit here and meditate." Otoko's step faltered as they started down the path. "I know I couldn't possibly paint them. They *are* abstract—maybe you've caught something with your reckless sketching."

Keiko took her arm. "Let's go home and play dolphin."

"Play dolphin? What on earth do you mean?"

Keiko laughed mischievously and headed off to the left toward a bamboo grove. It looked like the beautiful grove seen in photographs of the temple garden.

Otoko's expression seemed more strained than unhappy. As she walked along the edge of the grove, Keiko called to her, and came up and tapped her on the back. "Have you been hypnotized by that stone garden?"

"No, but I'd like to come here and do nothing but look at it for days and days."

"They're just stones, aren't they?" Her face was as bright and youthful as ever. "I'm sure you see a kind of power and mossy beauty radiating out of them, the way you look at them. But stones are stones. . . . I remember an essay by a haiku poet, something about looking at the sea day after day, and then moving to Kyoto and understanding what a stone garden really means."

"The sea in a stone garden? Of course if you think of the ocean, or great crags and cliffs, a stone arrangement in a garden is only man-made. Anyway, I'm afraid I couldn't paint this one."

"But it *is* only man-made! It's abstract. I feel as if I can do it in my own style, and use any color I please." After a moment she said: "When did they begin making stone gardens?"

"I don't know, probably not till the fourteenth century."

"And how old were the stones?"

"I have no idea."

"Would you like your pictures to last even longer?"

"I could never hope for that." Otoko looked troubled. "But don't you think that even this garden, or the garden of the Katsura Palace, has changed a great deal over the centuries? Trees grow and die, storms ravage it, and the like. Though probably the stone arrangements haven't changed much."

"Otoko, maybe it's best if everything changes and disappears!" Keiko exclaimed. "By now my tea-field picture must be torn to shreds, because of that night at Enoshima."

"But it was such a marvelous picture."

"Was it?"

"Keiko, do you intend to take all your best work to Mr. Oki?"

"Yes . . . until I finish getting revenge."

"I've told you I don't want to hear any more about revenge!"

"I understand," said Keiko cheerfully. "What I don't understand is my own spitefulness. Or is it feminine pride? Or jealousy?"

"Jealousy?" Otoko repeated in a low voice, grasping one of Keiko's fingers.

"Deep in your heart you're still in love with him. And he keeps you hidden deep in his own heart too. I could tell already on New Year's Eve."

Otoko was silent.

"I suppose even a woman's hatred is a kind of love."

"Keiko, how can you say a thing like that, here of all places?"

"To me, that stone garden symbolizes the powerful feelings of the men who made it. Yet I can't understand now what was in their hearts. It's taken centuries for the stones to get that patina, but I wonder how they looked when the garden was new."

"I think I'd be disillusioned."

"If I painted it, I'd use any shape and color I liked, and show those stones as if they had just been planted."

"Perhaps you *could* paint it."

"Otoko, that stone garden will last far, far longer than you or I!"

"Of course." As she spoke, Otoko felt a sudden chill. "Still, it won't last forever."

"If I'm with you I don't care if my pictures are short-lived, or even destroyed right away."

"That's because you're young."

"In fact, I'd be delighted if Mrs. Oki tore up my tea-field painting. I'd know she felt overwhelmed by emotion." She paused. "My pictures aren't worth taking seriously."

"That's not true."

"I have no real talent, and I don't want to leave anything to posterity. All I want is to be with you. I'd have been happy just to do your housework—and yet you've been willing to teach me to paint."

Otoko was taken aback. "Is that how you felt?"

"Deep down."

"But you do have talent! Sometimes it astonishes me."

"Like children's drawings? Mine were always being put up on the classroom wall."

"You're much more creative than I am. I often envy you. So please don't talk such nonsense."

"Very well." Keiko nodded gracefully. "As long as I can stay with you, I'll do my best. Let's change the subject."

"You do understand?"

Again Keiko nodded. "If you won't abandon me."

"How could I?" said Otoko. "But still . . . "

"But still what?"

"A woman has marriage, and children."

"Oh, that!" Keiko laughed. "*I* don't have them!"

"That's my fault. I'm sorry." Otoko turned away, her head drooping, and plucked a leaf from a tree. She walked on in silence.

"Otoko, women are pitiful creatures, aren't they? A young man would never love a sixty-year-old woman, but sometimes even teen-age girls fall in love with a man in his fifties or sixties. Not just because they want to get something out of it. . . . Isn't that right?" There was no reply. "Really, a man like Mr. Oki is a hopeless case. He thought I was just a slut."

Otoko paled.

"And then at the critical moment I heard myself calling your name—and he couldn't do another thing! . . . It was as if I'd been insulted as a woman because of you."

Otoko felt weak in the knees. Finally she asked: "At Enoshima?"

"Yes."

Somehow Otoko was unable to protest.

The taxi arrived at their temple. They went to sit in the studio together.

"I suppose you might say I was saved by that." Keiko could not help blushing. "Shall I have his baby for you?"

Suddenly she felt a stinging slap on the cheek. It brought tears to her eyes.

"Ah, that's good," she said. "Do it again!"

Otoko was trembling.

"Do it again!" Keiko repeated.

"Keiko!"

"It wouldn't be my baby. I want it to be yours. I'd bear it, and present it to you. I want to steal your baby from Mr. Oki——"

Again Otoko's slap stung her cheek. Keiko began sobbing. "Otoko, no matter how much you love him, you can't have his child anymore. You can't! I could have one without any feelings. It'd be as if you bore it yourself."

"Keiko——" Otoko went out on the veranda and kicked a cage of fireflies into the garden with her bare foot.

All the fireflies seemed to glow at once. A greenish-white light was streaming out as the cage landed on a patch of moss. The sky was clouding at the end of a long summer day, and an evening haze had begun to hover faintly over the garden, but it was still daylight. It seemed unlikely that the fireflies could have glowed so brilliantly;

perhaps she had only imagined the light streaming out of the cage, perhaps it had been conjured up by her own feelings. She stood there rigidly as if paralyzed and stared unblinking at the firefly cage lying on its side on the moss.

Keiko's sobbing stopped. Still half-reclining on the matted floor, propped up by her right arm, she watched Otoko from behind. For a time Otoko's rigidity seemed to be making her own body rigid.

But then Omiyo came in, and announced that the bath was ready.

"Thank you," said Otoko, her voice catching in her throat. She felt the moist chill of perspiration on her breast and the unpleasant dampness of her kimono under its wide obi. "Sticky, isn't it?" she went on, without turning. "Maybe the rainy season isn't over yet. . . . I'm glad you drew a bath."

Omiyo had been a maid at the temple for the past six years, and she also took care of Otoko's quarters. A hard worker, she did everything from housecleaning and laundry to washing dishes, even preparing occasional meals. Although Otoko liked to cook and was good at it, she would become too engrossed in painting. Keiko herself had a surprising knack for creating the subtle flavors of Kyoto cuisine, but she was inclined to be unreliable. Thus they often made do with simple dishes turned out by Omiyo. Since there were two other women at the temple—the master's young bride and his mother— Omiyo was free to spend most of her time taking care of

Otoko's needs. She was in her early fifties, small and pudgy, her wrists and ankles so plump the deep folds of flesh looked as if they had been tied with a string.

Buxom and cheerful as ever, Omiyo looked out at the firefly cage. "Miss Ueno, were you letting them drink the evening dew?" She went along the steppingstones to the cage and bent over to set it upright. She seemed to think it had been put in the garden intentionally.

By the time Omiyo stood up and looked toward the veranda Otoko had disappeared into the bathroom, and she found herself facing Keiko. There was a piercing gleam in Keiko's moist eyes, and in spite of her pallor one of her cheeks was red. Omiyo lowered her gaze again and asked if anything was wrong.

Keiko did not answer. She got up, her expression unchanged. She could hear water running in the bathroom. Otoko must be cooling down the hot bath water.

Standing before the mirror on the studio wall Keiko touched up her makeup with cosmetics from her handbag and then combed her hair with a little silver comb. A full-length mirror and a vanity with a winged mirror were in the dressing room next to the bathroom, but she hesitated to go in, since Otoko had undressed there. Keiko took the first unlined kimono she found from the top drawer of a chest, changed into fresh undergarments, and put on the kimono, slipping her long undersleeves through its sleeves and trying to adjust the front. But her hands were clumsy. Just then Otoko's name came to her lips. Glancing down at the kimono, Keiko saw Otoko in the dyed pattern of its sleeves and skirt.

Otoko had designed it for her. Its pattern of summer flowers seemed too boldly abstract to be one of Otoko's paintings; you could tell they were morning glories, but they were dreamlike flowers, their colors shaded in the latest fashion. It seemed very cool and youthful. Probably Otoko had designed it about the time she and Keiko became inseparable.

"Miss Sakami, are you going out?" Omiyo called to her from the next room.

"What are you looking at?" said Keiko, without turning. "Maybe you ought to come in and do it for me!" It had occurred to her that Omiyo might be suspicious of her awkwardness in tying her undersash.

"Are you going out?" Omiyo repeated, after a moment.

"No, I'm not!" Taking up her kimono skirt in her right hand, with the obi over the other arm, Keiko went toward the dressing room. "Bring me a pair of stockings, please," she said brusquely to Omiyo.

Otoko heard her footsteps and thought Keiko had come to join her in the tub. "The water's just right!" she called. But Keiko was standing in front of the full-length mirror, still tying her undersash. She jerked it so tight it almost cut into her flesh.

Omiyo brought in the stockings, put them down, and left.

"Come on in!" Otoko called again. As she sat soaking in water up to her breasts she watched the cedar door to the dressing room. But Keiko did not open it. There was not even the sound of rustling clothes.

Struck by a sudden fear that Keiko might be reluctant to bathe with her, Otoko grasped the edge of the tub, pulled herself out of the water, and stepped down on the bathroom floor.

Was Keiko hesitant to let Otoko see her body, after having spent a night with Oki?

It was over two weeks ago that she had returned from Tokyo. Since then, she had often bathed with Otoko, and had never betrayed any shame at being seen naked. Yet it was only today, at the stone garden, that Keiko had unexpectedly confessed. What she said had seemed extraordinary.

For years Otoko had been discovering almost daily what a strange young girl Keiko was. No doubt she herself had helped to intensify that strangeness. It could not be said that Otoko was entirely responsible, but certainly she had fanned the flames within her.

As Otoko waited in the bathroom, drops of cold sweat gathered on her forehead. "Keiko, aren't you coming in?" she asked.

"No."

"You're not taking a bath?"

"No."

"Not even to sponge off?"

"I don't need to." After a pause, Keiko's voice rang out clearly. "Otoko, I'm sorry. Please forgive me."

"Forgive *me* . . . " Otoko echoed. "I'm the one to blame. I apologize."

Keiko said nothing.

"What are you doing? Are you just standing there?"

"I'm tying my obi."

"Did you say you're tying your obi?" Suspicious, Otoko hastily dried herself and went into the dressing room. Keiko was immaculate in a fresh kimono.

"My, are you going somewhere?"

"Yes."

"But where?"

"I don't know," said Keiko, a tinge of sadness in her shining eyes.

Otoko slipped a light bath robe over her shoulders, as if embarrassed by her own nakedness. "I'll go with you."

"All right."

"Do you mind?"

"Of course not." Keiko turned away. Her face was reflected in the full-length mirror. "I'll be waiting for you."

"I won't be long. Just let me in there, please." Otoko went past Keiko and sat down at the dressing table. She looked at her in the mirror. "How about Kiyamachi? Ofusa's place. Call and ask for a table on the balcony, or a little room on the second floor—anything, really, as long as it looks out on the river. . . . If you can't get that, let's go somewhere else."

Keiko nodded. "First I'll bring you a glass of ice water."

"Do I look hot?"

"Yes."

"Don't worry, I won't get violent. . . . " Otoko shook

some lotion from a bottle onto the palm of her left hand.

The ice water Keiko brought sent a chill all the way down her throat.

Keiko had to go to the main residence of the temple to make her telephone call. When she came back Otoko was still hurrying to get dressed.

"Ofusa says we can have a balcony table until eight-thirty."

"Eight-thirty?" Otoko frowned. "Well, that will do. If we go right away we can have a leisurely dinner." Drawing the side mirrors of the vanity closer together, she leaned forward and looked at her hair. "I suppose I needn't redo it."

Keiko reached behind Otoko's obi and gently straightened the back seam of her kimono.

THE LOTUS
IN THE
FLAMES

There is a celebrated passage in the *Illustrated Sights of the Capital* about people enjoying summer evenings along the Kamo River: "Benches line the wide strand, and balconies stretch out over the river banks from the houses of pleasure on both east and west, their lamps like stars reflected in the water. The dark purple kerchiefs of young Kabuki actors flutter in the river breeze—these beautiful youths are shy in the bright moonlight, and seductively shade themselves with their fans, so gracefully that those who see them are too entranced to avert their gaze. Now the courtesans are at their most exquisite, promenading to north and to south, lovelier than the hibiscus and fragrant with rich perfumes. . . . " And then there were the comic story tellers, mimics, and other entertainers—"monkeys, wrestling dogs, trained horses, pillow jugglers, rope walkers who prance like fabulous beasts. You hear the boisterous piping of a street vendor's flute, the rush of a cooling waterfall in a jelly shop, the echo of tinkling glass wind chimes to invite the evening breeze. Rare birds of Japan and China, and wild beasts from the mountains, are gathered and put on show, and people of all kinds crowd together to feast and drink by the river."

In 1690 the poet Basho also came here, and wrote: "What is called enjoying a summer evening by the river goes on from sunset till the last glimmer of the moon at dawn. Balconies line the river banks for drinking and feasting. Women knot their obi in splendid bows, men come turned out in long cloaks, priests and old gentlemen mingle with the crowd, even young apprentices of coopers and blacksmiths sing and make merry as carefree as can be. Truly a scene of the Capital!

> *The river breeze———*
> *Out in a thin russet kimono*
> *On a summer evening."*

After the Meiji era the river bottom was deepened, and electric trains to Osaka began running along the east bank. It was the end of the evenings by the river "on a strand dotted with booths for a variety of shows, acrobatics, rarities and curiosities, and the like, all lighted up by lanterns, lamps, and bonfires, as bright as day"—the end, too, of the merry-go-rounds and tightwire performances added toward the close of Meiji. Only the balconies along Kiyamachi and Ponto-cho were reminiscent of the old summer evenings by the river. Of all she had read about those evenings, what particularly lingered in Otoko's memory was the passage about the young Kabuki actors who joined the throngs on the moonlit strand, their dark purple kerchiefs fluttering in the river breeze. "These beautiful youths are shy in the bright moonlight, and seductively shade themselves with their fans . . . " Alluring images would drift into Otoko's mind.

The first time she saw Keiko she was reminded of those beautiful youths.

Again Otoko recalled it, sitting there on the balcony of Ofusa's tea house. Probably the young Kabuki actors were more feminine, more seductive, than the boyish Keiko of their first meeting. As usual, it occurred to her that she herself had made that girl into the young woman she was today. "Keiko," she said, "do you remember when you first called on me?"

"Must you bring that up again?"

"I felt as if a young sorceress had appeared."

Keiko took Otoko's hand, lifted it to her mouth and, glancing up at her, nibbled on the little finger. Then she whispered: "It was a hazy spring evening, and you seemed to float in the pale bluish haze that hung over the garden."

Those had been Otoko's words. Otoko had told her that in the evening haze she looked all the more like a young sorceress. Keiko had not forgotten.

Once again the remembered words had been spoken. Keiko knew very well that they tormented Otoko, made her blame herself and regret her attachment, and yet gave that attachment an even more uncanny power over her.

Paper lamps stood at each corner of the tea house

balcony next to Ofusa's, where three geisha, two of them young girls, were entertaining a single guest. The guest was a plump, balding, youngish man who kept glancing out at the river and nodding indifferently as the girls tried to make conversation. Was he waiting for the night or for a companion? The lanterns were already lit, but hardly seemed necessary in the early dusk.

The two balconies were almost within touching distance. Like the others jutting out over the narrow stream along the walled west bank of the Kamo, they were not only roofless but without blinds. You could see all the way down to the farthest balcony. The row of open balconies gave the feeling of the coolness of a river bank.

Unconcerned by the lack of privacy, Keiko bit down hard on Otoko's little finger. The pain darted through her, but Otoko did not flinch. Keiko's tongue played with the tip of the finger. Then she let it fall from her mouth, and said: "You took a bath, so it's not the least bit salty."

The wide view of the Kamo River and the hills beyond the city soothed Otoko's anger, and as her feelings calmed she began to think that she was to blame even for the Keiko that went to stay overnight with Oki.

Keiko had just graduated from high school when she first came to Otoko's studio. She said she had seen her pictures at a show in Tokyo and photographs of her in a magazine, and had fallen in love with her.

That year one of Otoko's paintings had won a prize at a Kyoto exhibition and, partly because of its subject, had become well known.

It was a painting of two young geisha playing scissors-paper-and-stone, based on a trick photograph of around 1880. The photograph showed a double image of the famous Gion geisha Okayo: the girl on the right, the fingers of both hands outstretched, was almost full face; and the other, fists clenched, was turned slightly aside. Otoko liked the composition of the hands and the contrasting postures and facial expressions of the two geisha. The girl with fingers outstretched held her thumb extended and her fingers curved back. Otoko liked the identical costumes, too (though it was impossible to tell their colors from the photograph), and the old-fashioned, large-patterned design that ran from shoulder to hem. There was also a square wooden brazier between the two figures, along with an iron kettle and a sake bottle, but because they would have cluttered the picture Otoko omitted them.

Her own painting showed the same young geisha, doubled, playing scissors-paper-and-stone. She wanted to give an uneasy feeling that the one girl was two, the two one, or perhaps neither one nor two. Even the dated trick photograph had something of that feeling. To avoid ending up with a merely clever notion, Otoko took great pains over the faces. The decorative pattern of the clothing that looked so bulky in the photograph was a help, and set off the four hands vividly. Although the painting was not an exact copy, many Kyoto people must have recognized at a glance that it was based on a photograph of an early Meiji geisha.

A Tokyo art dealer who was interested in the geisha painting came to see Otoko. He arranged to exhibit some of her smaller works in Tokyo. That was when Keiko saw them—purely by chance, since she had never heard of the Kyoto artist Ueno Otoko.

No doubt it was because of the geisha painting—and the beauty of the painter—that Otoko had been featured by a weekly magazine. She was taken here and there around Kyoto by a staff photographer and a reporter, for shot after shot of her. Or rather Otoko took them, since they wanted to go to the places she liked. The result was a special picture story that covered three of the magazine's large pages. It included a photograph of the geisha painting and a close-up of Otoko, but most of the pictures were scenes of Kyoto, with Otoko for human interest. Possibly their aim had been to find places off the beaten path, by having a Kyoto artist as a guide. Not that Otoko felt herself unfairly used—she realized she was given three full pages—but the backgrounds were certainly not the ordinary "views of Kyoto."

Keiko, however, unaware that these were the hidden charms of the city, saw only the beauty of Otoko. She was fascinated.

So Keiko had appeared out of a pale bluish haze and begged to be taken in to study painting with her. The fervor of that appeal shocked Otoko. And then suddenly Keiko's arms were around her, and she seemed to be in the embrace of a young sorceress. It was like an unexpected throb of desire.

But Otoko demurred and asked if her father and mother knew. "Otherwise I can't give you an answer. I'm sure you understand."

"Both my parents are dead," said Keiko. "I can make up my own mind."

Otoko looked at her quizzically. "Don't you have an aunt or uncle, or any brothers or sisters?"

"I'm a burden to my brother and his wife. Now that they have a baby, I seem to be more trouble than ever."

"Because of the baby?"

"I'm fond of it, naturally. They don't like my way of cuddling it."

Four or five days after Keiko settled down with her, Otoko received a letter from the brother saying that she was a wild, headstrong girl, and probably would not even make a good maid, but that he hoped Otoko would take her in. Keiko's clothing and other belongings also arrived. They gave the impression that she came from a well-to-do family.

Otoko soon realized that there must have been something abnormal about the way Keiko cuddled the baby.

Was it a week after Keiko had come? She had coaxed Otoko to do her hair for her, any way she liked, but in handling it Otoko happened to tug a few strands. "Pull harder!" Keiko had said. "Grab it up so that I hang by it!"

Otoko let go. Twisting around toward her, Keiko pressed her lips and teeth to the back of Otoko's hand. Then she said: "Miss Ueno, how old were you at your first kiss?"

"Really, now!"

"I was three. I remember distinctly. He was an uncle on my mother's side, about thirty, I suppose. But I liked him, and once when he was sitting alone in the parlor I toddled right up and kissed him. He was so startled he clapped his hand to his mouth."

There on the balcony beside the river Otoko recalled the story of that childish kiss. The lips that had kissed a man at three now belonged to her, and had just held her little finger.

"I remember the spring rain the first time you took me to Mt. Arashi," said Keiko.

"So do I."

"And the woman at the noodle shop."

A few days after Keiko's first visit Otoko took her around to see the Golden Pavilion, the Moss Temple, the Ryoanji Temple, and then Mt. Arashi. They had gone into a noodle shop on the river bank near the Togetsu Bridge. The old woman at the shop said she was sorry it was raining.

"I like the rain," Otoko replied. "It's a nice spring rain."

"Oh, thank you, ma'am," said the woman politely. She made a little bow.

Keiko looked at Otoko, and whispered: "Was she speaking for the weather?"

"What?" The woman's remark had seemed quite natural to Otoko. "Yes, I imagine so. For the weather."

"That's interesting," Keiko went on. "I like the idea of saying thank you on behalf of the weather. Is that what Kyoto people do?"

To be sure, you could interpret her remark that way.

Apologizing to them for the rain was natural enough. But Otoko's reply had not been from sheer politeness; she really did like Mt. Arashi in a gentle spring rain. The old woman thanked her for that. She seemed to be speaking for the weather, or for Mt. Arashi in the rain. It was also a natural greeting from someone who had a shop there, but to Keiko it had sounded odd.

"Marvelous noodles, aren't they?" said Keiko. "I like this place." Their taxi driver had recommended it. Because of the rain Otoko had hired the taxi for half a day.

Even though it was the cherry blossom season, surprisingly few people were willing to come here in the rain, which was another reason why Otoko liked it. Yet the misty spring rain softened the outline of the mountain across the river and made it even more beautiful. So gentle was the rain that they hardly knew they were getting wet as they strolled back toward the car, not even bothering to put up their umbrella. The slender threads of rain vanished into the river without a ripple. Cherry blossoms were intermingled with young green leaves, the colors of the budding trees all delicately subdued in the rain.

The Moss Temple and Ryoanji were also lovely in the spring rain. At the Moss Temple a single red camellia lay atop little white andromeda blossoms scattered over the wet moss, red on white on green. The perfectly formed camellia lay face up as if it had bloomed there afloat. And the rain-wet stones of the stone garden at Ryoanji glistened in all their hues.

"When you use a vase of old Iga ware in the tea ceremony, you moisten it first, you know," said Otoko. "It's the same effect." But Keiko was not familiar with Iga ware, nor did she have any particular feeling for the colors of the stone garden before her.

However, once Otoko had pointed them out to her, she was impressed by the raindrops glittering in the young pines along the path through the temple compound. Each needle was like a flower stem with a single droplet of rain clinging to its very tip; the trees seemed all abloom with dew flowers. Easily overlooked, they were subtle blossoms of the spring rain. The maples and other trees also had raindrops on their budding leaves.

Raindrops clinging to the tips of pine needles could be seen anywhere, but it was the first time Keiko had really noticed them, and so they seemed to belong to Kyoto. The raindrops on the pine needles and the greeting of the old woman at the noodle shop were among Keiko's first impressions of Kyoto. Not only was the city new to her, she was seeing it with Otoko.

"I wonder how the woman at the noodle shop is," said Keiko. "We haven't been back to Mt. Arashi since."

"That's true. But I like it best of all in winter, when the pools in the river look deep and cold. Let's go out then."

"Must we wait till winter?"

"Winter will be here soon enough."

"It won't be soon at all! It's not even midsummer, let alone fall."

Otoko laughed. "We can go any time! We can go tomorrow."

"Let's. I'll tell the noodle shop woman I like Mt. Arashi in the heat of summer and she'll probably thank me. For the hot weather."

"And for Mt. Arashi."

Keiko looked out at the river. "Otoko, by winter there won't be any more of these couples walking along the banks."

Many young people were out on the two levees used as promenades that separated the Kamo from the stream under the balconies and from the canal along its eastern bank. Only a few were with children—almost all of them seemed to be lovers. Young couples were walking close together, or sitting at the water's edge leaning against each other. As dusk gathered, their numbers grew.

"Of course it's much too cold here in winter," said Otoko.

"I doubt it would last till winter."

"What would last?"

"Their love. Some of them will stop wanting to see each other by then."

"Is that what's on your mind?" Keiko nodded. "Why must you worry about that, at your age?"

"Because I'm not a fool like you, for twenty years loving someone who spoiled your life!"

Otoko was silent.

"Even though Mr. Oki deserted you, you've refused to recognize it."

"Please don't talk like that." As Otoko turned away, Keiko reached out to smooth up a few stray hairs at the back of Otoko's neck.

"Otoko, why don't you desert me?"

"What!"

"I'm the only person you *can* desert. So go ahead."

"Whatever can you mean?" Otoko seemed to parry her lightly, but looked straight into her eyes. She ran her fingertips over the hairs Keiko had smoothed.

"I mean the way Mr. Oki deserted you," said Keiko tenaciously, peering into Otoko's eyes. "Though apparently you've never been willing to think about it that way."

"Must you use a word like 'desert'?"

"It's best to be precise." There was a malicious glint in her eye. "What would you call it?"

"We parted."

"But you didn't! Even now he's there within you, and you're within him."

"Keiko, what are you trying to tell me? I can't understand you."

"Today I thought you were going to abandon me."

"But I apologized, didn't I?"

"*I* apologized to *you*."

Otoko had brought her here to Kiyamachi for a reconciliation, but perhaps that was no longer possible. Evidently it was Keiko's temperament to be dissatisfied with a placid love, so she was always crossing Otoko, or quarreling with her, or sulking. Still, her confession to having spent the night with Oki had wounded Otoko. The Keiko who seemed to be under her control had turned into some strange creature attacking her. Keiko had said she would take revenge on Oki for her sake, but to Otoko it seemed Keiko was taking revenge on her. Also, she felt a new horror toward Oki as a man. How dare he trifle with her protégée, when he must have other women as well?

"You aren't going to abandon me?" Keiko asked.

"If you keep insisting, I will! That would be best for you anyway."

"Stop it! That's not what I meant." Keiko shook her head. "I wasn't thinking of my own good. As long as I'm with you . . . "

"Being apart from me would certainly be best for you." Otoko was trying to speak calmly.

"Are you already apart from me, in your heart?"

"Of course not!"

"I'm glad! I felt so wretched, wondering if you were through with me."

"But that was your idea."

"Mine? . . . You think I'd leave you?"

Otoko said nothing.

"Never in my life!" Keiko burst out, and again grasped Otoko's little finger and bit it.

"Ouch!" Otoko shrank back. "That hurt, you know!"

"I meant it to."

Dinner arrived. As the waitress arranged the dishes Keiko turned primly away and sat gazing at a cluster of lights on Mt. Hiei. Otoko made conversation with the waitress, keeping one hand over the other. She was afraid the teeth marks were visible.

When they were alone again Keiko looked down at her soup bowl, took a morsel of eel with her chopsticks, and said: "But you really ought to desert me."

"You *are* stubborn, aren't you?"

"I'm the kind of girl that's deserted by her lover. Do you think I'm stubborn?"

Otoko asked herself if women were more stubborn toward each other than toward men, and felt the needle prick of the same old guilty thought. Her finger was still stinging too, as if pierced by a needle. Had she herself taught Keiko to inflict pain?

One day, not long after they began living together, Keiko had come running in from the kitchen, saying the oil in the frying pan had spattered.

"Did you get burned?"

"It stings!" Keiko thrust her hand out to Otoko. The tip of one finger was red. Otoko took the hand.

"It doesn't look bad," she said, and quickly stuck the finger in her mouth. Startled by the touch of her tongue on it, she took it out again. This time Keiko put the finger in her own mouth.

"Does it help to lick it?"

"Keiko, what about your frying pan?"

"I forgot!" She ran back to the kitchen.

Later—when had it been?—Otoko somehow began toying with her at night, pressing her lips on Keiko's eyelids, or nibbling at her sensitive ears until she squirmed and moaned. That led Otoko on.

All the while Otoko remembered that long, long ago Oki had toyed with her the same way. Perhaps because she was so young, he had been in no hurry to kiss her on the mouth. As she felt his lips again and again on her forehead, her eyelids, her cheeks, she was lulled into utter submission. Keiko was two or three years older, and of the same sex, but she responded even more quickly. Otoko soon found her irresistible. However, the thought that she was repeating Oki's old caresses made her feel a choking sense of guilt. But it also made her quiver with vitality.

"Don't do that. Please!" Yet as Keiko spoke she nestled her bare breast against Otoko's. "Isn't your body the same as mine?"

Otoko drew back.

Keiko clung to her more closely. "Isn't it? Just the same as mine!" She waited a moment. "It really is, you know."

Otoko suspected that she was not a virgin. Keiko's sudden verbal thrusts were still unfamiliar to her.

"We're not the same," Otoko murmured, as Keiko's hand came groping for her breast. The hand moved without hesitation, but there seemed to be shyness in its touch. "Don't do that!" Otoko clutched Keiko's hand.

"You're not being fair!" Now there was strength in Keiko's fingers.

Years ago, at fifteen, when she felt Oki's hand on her breasts Otoko had said: "Don't do that. Please!" Exactly those words had appeared in his novel. She would probably have remembered them anyway, but because they were in the book they seemed to have taken on a life of their own.

And yet Keiko had said the same thing. Was it because she had read *A Girl of Sixteen*? Was this what any girl would say?

The novel also had a description of Otoko's breasts, along with something Oki had said about the bliss of touching them.

Because Otoko had never nursed a baby, her nipples still retained their rich color. Even after twenty years that color had not faded. But since her early thirties her breasts had begun to shrink.

Probably Keiko had noticed their slackness in the bath, and made sure of it when she touched them. Otoko wondered if she would mention it, but she never did. Nor was anything said when Otoko's breasts responded to Keiko's caresses by steadily becoming fuller. Keiko's silence was odd, since she must have considered it a victory.

Sometimes Otoko felt that the swelling of her breasts was morbid and evil, sometimes she felt terribly ashamed; above all, she was astonished by the way her body, at almost forty, was changing. That was very different from what she had felt at fifteen, when the shape of her breasts changed under Oki's caresses, and again at sixteen, when she was pregnant.

After her parting from Oki no one had touched her breasts for over two decades. Meanwhile her youth, and her chance to marry, had passed. It was the hand of another woman—Keiko—that had touched them once again.

Still, Otoko had had many opportunities for love and

marriage since coming to Kyoto with her mother. But she had avoided them. As soon as she realized that a man was in love with her, memories of Oki were revived. Rather than mere recollections, they were her reality. When she parted from Oki she thought she would never marry. Distraught by sorrow, she could hardly plan ahead to the next day, much less to the distant future. But the thought of never marrying had crept into her mind, and in time it became an inflexible resolution.

Of course Otoko's mother hoped for her to marry. She had moved to Kyoto to keep her away from Oki, and to calm her, not with the intention of settling down permanently. Even in Kyoto her anxiety over her daughter remained. The first time she brought up a marriage proposal was when Otoko was nineteen. It was at the Nembutsu Temple in Adashino, deep in the Saga plain, on the night of the Ceremony of the Thousand Lights.

Otoko noticed tears in her mother's eyes as she looked at the thousand lights burning before the countless little weathered gravestones, memorials to the unmourned dead, that stood in rows across the gravel bed symbolizing the children's Limbo. A sense of mortality hung in the air. The feeble candle flames flickering there in the dusk made the gravestones seem all the more melancholy.

It was dark as they walked back together along a country road.

"My, but it's lonely," her mother said. "Don't you feel lonely, Otoko?" This time the word "lonely" seemed to have a different meaning. She began talking about a marriage proposal for Otoko that had come by way of a friend in Tokyo.

"I feel guilty toward you because I can't marry," said Otoko.

"There's no such thing as a woman who can't marry!"

"But there is."

"If you don't, we'll both be among the unmourned dead."

"I don't know what that means."

"They're the ones who have no relatives left to mourn them."

"I know, but I can't imagine what *that* would mean." She paused. "You're dead, after all."

"It's not just when you're dead. A woman without husband or children must be like that even while she's still alive. Suppose I didn't have you. You're still young, but . . . " Her mother hesitated. "You often paint pictures of your baby, don't you? How long do you expect to go on doing that?"

Otoko did not reply.

Her mother told her all she knew about the proposed marriage partner, a bank clerk. "If you'd like to meet him, let's make a visit to Tokyo."

"What do you suppose I see before me as I listen to you?" Otoko asked.

"You're seeing something?"

"Iron bars. I see the iron bars on the windows of that psychiatric ward."

Her mother was silenced.

Otoko received several more proposals while her mother was alive.

"It's no good thinking about Mr. Oki," her mother said, urging her to marry. It was more an appeal than a warning. "There's nothing you can do. Waiting for Mr. Oki is like waiting for the past—time and the river won't flow backward."

"I'm not waiting for anyone," Otoko replied.

"You just keep thinking of him? You can't forget him?"

"It's not that."

"Are you sure? . . . You were only a child when he seduced you—an innocent child, if ever there was one—so maybe that's why it's left a scar. I used to hate him for being cruel to such a child!"

Otoko remembered her mother's words. She wondered if it was because of her youth and innocence that she had had such a love. Perhaps that explained her blind, insatiable passion. When a spasm gripped her and she bit his shoulder she would not even realize that blood was flowing.

Long after separating from Oki, she was shocked to read in *A Girl of Sixteen* that on his way to meet her he would be trying to decide how to make love to her, and that he usually did exactly as he had planned. She found it appalling that a man's heart would "throb with joy as he walked along thinking about it." To a spontaneous young girl like Otoko it had been inconceivable that a man would plan in advance his lovemaking techniques, their sequence, and the like. She accepted whatever he did, gave whatever he asked. Her youth made her all the more unquestioning. Oki had described her as an extraordinary girl, a woman among women. Thanks to her, he wrote, he had experienced all the ways of making love.

When she read that, Otoko burned with humiliation. But she could not suppress her lively memories of his lovemaking; her body tensed and began to quiver. Finally the tension was released, and delight and satisfaction spread through her whole body. Her past love had come back to life.

It was not only the vision of the iron bars of a hospital window that Otoko saw on her way home along the dark road from the Ceremony of the Thousand Lights. She also saw herself lying in Oki's embrace.

If he had not written about it, perhaps that vision of herself would not have remained alive for so many years.

Otoko had paled with jealous anger and despair when Keiko told her that at the critical moment in Oki's embrace she had called her name—"and he couldn't do another thing!" But beneath those emotions she felt that Oki had also remembered *her*. Had not a vision of her lying in his arms come sharply before him at that instant?

As time passed, the memory of their embrace was gradually becoming purified within Otoko, changing from physical to spiritual. She herself was not now pure; nor was Oki, in all likelihood. Yet their long-ago embrace, as she now saw it, seemed pure. That memory—

herself and not herself, unreal and yet real—was a sacred vision sublimated from the memory of their mutual embrace.

When she recalled what he had taught her, and imitated it in making love to Keiko, she feared that the sacred vision might be stained or even destroyed. But it remained inviolate.

Keiko was in the habit of using a depilatory cream to remove hair from her legs and arms, and began to smear it on in Otoko's presence. At first she had done it in private. When Otoko would ask her about an odd smell coming from the bathroom, she would not reply. Otoko was unacquainted with depilatories, having never needed one.

Then she happened to see Keiko sitting with one knee drawn up, smoothing on the cream. Otoko frowned.

"Such a nasty smell! What is it?" When the hairs came out in the cream as it was being wiped off, Otoko covered her eyes. "Please don't do that! It makes my flesh crawl." She shivered and felt herself breaking out in goose pimples. "Do you have to do such a repulsive thing?"

"But doesn't everyone?"

Otoko was silent.

"Wouldn't it make your flesh crawl to touch a hairy skin?"

Still Otoko did not answer.

"I'm a woman, after all."

So she was doing it for Otoko. Even for another woman, Keiko wanted to have a woman's silky skin. Otoko felt oppressed both by her own sense of repug-

nance at seeing the hair removed and by the feelings that
Keiko's frankness had aroused. The acrid smell lingered
in her nostrils even after Keiko went to the bath to wash
off the rest of the cream.

When Keiko came back she pulled up her skirt and
stretched out a sleek milk-white leg. "Touch it and see.
It's all smooth now." Otoko glanced down, but did not
put out her hand. Keiko stroked her shin with her right
hand, and looked at Otoko as if wondering what could
be wrong. "Is something bothering you?" she asked.
Otoko avoided her eyes.

"Keiko, from now on please don't do it in front of
me."

"I never want to hide anything from you again. I have
no more secrets from you."

"Surely you needn't show me something I find offen-
sive."

"You'll get used to it. It's just like trimming toenails."

"You shouldn't do your nails in front of people either.
When you clip your nails you let them fly. . . . Cup your
hand so the clippings won't get away."

Keiko meekly agreed.

After that, however, Keiko neither flaunted nor concealed her efforts to remove hair from her arms and legs.
But Otoko never got used to it. Whether the depilatory
cream had been improved or Keiko had substituted a
different one, the smell was no longer quite so bad; still,
the whole process made Otoko queasy. She could not
bear to watch the shin and underarm hairs come out as
the cream was wiped away. She would leave the room.

Yet beneath her repugnance a flame flickered and vanished, and flickered up again. That small, distant flame was barely visible to her mind's eye, but so calm, so pure, that it was hard to believe it was a flicker of lust. It reminded her of Oki and herself all those years ago. Her queasiness at seeing Keiko remove hair had within it a feeling of contact between woman and woman, a direct pressure on her own skin; and her first reaction had been one of nausea. But when she thought of Oki the queasiness miraculously subsided.

In his embrace she had never had that feeling of queasiness; nor was she even aware of whether Oki himself was hairy. Did she lose her sense of reality? Now, with Keiko, she was even freer, she had developed a bold, middle-aged eroticism. It had amazed her to learn through Keiko that she had ripened as a woman during her long years alone. She feared that had her new lover been a man the vision she secretly guarded within her—the sacred vision of her love with Oki—would have vanished at his touch.

Otoko had failed in her early suicide attempt, but she always wished that she had died. Better still, she felt, to have died in childbirth—before she tried to kill herself, and before her own baby died. Yet as the months and years slipped by, these thoughts cleansed the wound she had received from Oki.

"You're more than I deserve. It's a love I never dreamed I'd find. Happiness like this is worth dying for. . . . " Even now Oki's words had not faded from her memory. The dialogue in his novel echoed them and seemed to have taken on a life apart from either Oki or herself. Perhaps the lovers of old were no more, but she had the nostalgic consolation, in the midst of her sadness, that their love was forever enshrined in a work of art.

Otoko's mother had left behind a razor she had used for shaving her face. Little as she needed it, Otoko would occasionally take it out—perhaps once a year, as if impelled by some memory—and shave the nape of her neck and the hairline at her forehead. One day when she saw Keiko begin to spread on that depilatory cream she suddenly announced: "Keiko, I'll shave you." She took her mother's razor out of the drawer of the dressing table.

As soon as she saw the razor Keiko exclaimed, "No, no, I'm afraid!" and fled from the room. Otoko pursued her all the more eagerly.

"It's not dangerous! Please, let me!"

Once caught, Keiko reluctantly allowed herself to be brought back to the dressing table. But when Otoko soaped her arm and applied the razor, she noticed with surprise that Keiko's fingers were trembling.

"Don't worry, it's perfectly safe. Just keep your arm steady."

However, she found Keiko's anxiety stimulating. It was a temptation. Her own body tensed, and strength seemed to flow into her shoulders.

"Maybe I'd better let the underarm go this time," said Otoko. "But your face won't be any trouble."

"Wait, let me catch my breath," Keiko begged.

Otoko shaved above her eyebrows and under her lip.
While the hairline around her forehead was being shaved
Keiko kept her eyes tight shut. Face tilted up, she rested
her head on Otoko's supporting hand. That long, slender throat caught Otoko's attention. It was a curiously
innocent-looking throat, delicate and shapely, glowing
with youth. Otoko held her razor still.

Keiko opened her eyes. "What's wrong?"

The thought had come to Otoko that if she thrust her
razor into this lovely throat, Keiko would die. At this
moment she could easily kill her with a single stroke
against the loveliest part of her body.

Her own slender, girlish throat had surely not been so
beautiful, but once when Oki's arm was around it she had
protested that he was strangling her. Then he had
squeezed even harder.

The choking sensation came back to her as she looked
at Keiko. She began to feel dizzy.

It was the only time Otoko shaved her. After that
Keiko always refused, and Otoko did not insist. When
she opened the drawer of the dressing table for a comb
or whatever, she would see her mother's razor. Sometimes it reminded her of that faint murderous impulse
that had flitted through her mind. If she *had* killed Keiko,
she herself would not have gone on living. Later that
impulse seemed like a vaguely familiar wraith. Was that
another time when she missed a chance to die?

Otoko realized that in that fleeting murderous impulse
lurked her old love for Oki. At the time Keiko had not

yet met him. She had not put herself between them.

Now that Otoko had heard about the night at Enoshima, that old love flared up ominously within her. Yet
in those flames she could see a single white lotus blossom. Their love was a dreamlike flower that not even
Keiko could stain.

The white lotus still there before her inner eye, Otoko
shifted her gaze to the lights of the Kiyamachi tea houses
reflected in the stream below. For some time she looked
down at them. Then she looked at the dark range of the
Eastern Hills, beyond Gion. The softly rounded hills
were peaceful, but the darkness within them seemed to
be flowing secretly toward her. The headlights of automobiles coming and going along the opposite bank,
the couples on the promenades, the lamps and people on
the balconies lining this side of the river—all these
Otoko saw without really seeing them, as the night scene
of the Eastern Hills spread out in her mind.

I'll go ahead with my *Ascension of an Infant,* Otoko told
herself. If I don't paint it right away, I may never be able
to. It's already on the verge of turning into something
different . . . losing all the love and sadness. Was this
rush of feeling because she saw the lotus in the flames?
It began to seem as if Keiko were the lotus. Why did the
white lotus bloom in fire? Why did it not wither away?

"Keiko," she said suddenly, "are you in a good humor
again?"

"If you are." Keiko's tone seemed coquettish.

"Tell me, which of your sadnesses have been
deepest?" Otoko asked.

"I'm not sure," she answered casually, "I've had so many I can't say. I'll try to remember all of them, and let you know. But my sadnesses are brief."

"Are they?"

"Yes."

Otoko looked hard at her. Speaking as calmly as possible, she said: "There's one thing I want to ask of you tonight. Please don't go to Kamakura again."

"Do you mean to see Mr. Oki? Or his son?"

Her question stabbed Otoko. "Either one, of course!"

"I only went to get revenge for you!"

"Are you still talking like that? What a frightening girl you are!" Otoko's expression changed, and she shut her eyes as if to hold back unforeseen tears.

"You're such a coward. . . . " Keiko rose and went behind Otoko. She pressed down her shoulders with both hands, and then played with her ears. As Otoko sat there vacantly, she could hear the murmur of the flowing stream.

STRANDS OF
BLACK HAIR

We have a visitor, dear!" Fumiko called to Oki from the kitchen where she was preparing breakfast. "A great big Mrs. Mouse is honoring us, hiding under the stove." Sometimes his wife taunted him by using exaggeratedly polite language.

"Is that so?"

"She even seems to have her little offspring along."

"Oh?"

"Really, you ought to come see. . . . The baby mouse just peeped out, and he has the sweetest face."

"Hmm."

"He looked at me with beautiful sparkling black eyes."

Oki said nothing. The pungent aroma of *miso* soup drifted into the dining room, where he was reading the morning newspaper.

"Now the rain's leaking in! Right into the kitchen. Can you hear it, dear?"

It was raining when he woke up, but now it had become a heavy downpour. The wind that swayed the pines and bamboos on the hill had veered around to the east and was driving the rain in from that side.

"How could I, with all the rain and wind?"

"Won't you come and look?"

"Mmm."

"Those poor little raindrops—hurled against the roof tiles, and squeezed through cracks, like teardrops weeping in on us . . . "

"You'll have me crying too."

"Let's set the wire trap tonight. I think it's up on the closet shelf. Will you get it down for me later, please?"

"Are you sure you want to catch Mrs. Mouse and her sweet little offspring in a trap?" said Oki mildly, without looking up from his newspaper.

"And what about the leak?"

"How bad is it? Isn't that just the way the wind is blowing? Tomorrow I'll get up on the roof and see."

"That's dangerous for an old man. I can have Taichiro climb up."

"Who's an old man?"

"You retire at fifty-five in most businesses, don't you?"

"I'm glad to hear that. Maybe I should retire too."

"Do, whenever you please."

"I wonder what the retirement age is in the novel business."

"The day you die."

"Indeed!"

"I'm sorry," Fumiko apologized, and then added in

her usual tone: "I only meant you can go on writing a long, long time."

"That's not a very pleasant outlook, especially with a nagging wife. It's like being prodded by the devil's pitchfork."

"Really! When did I ever nag you?"

"You can be a nuisance, you know."

"What do you mean by that?"

"Well, jealousy, for example."

"All women are jealous, but you taught me long ago that it's a bitter, dangerous medicine . . . a double-edged sword."

"To wound your partner and yourself."

"No matter what, I'm too old for double suicide or divorce."

"Old couples getting divorced are bad enough, but there's nothing sadder than when they commit suicide together. It must make an old person feel agitated to see such articles in the papers. Even more so than the way young people feel about the suicide of young lovers."

"That's because you were agitated about double suicide once yourself, a long time ago. . . . Anyway, you didn't let your young girl friend know you wanted to die with her. Maybe you should have. She killed herself, but she never dreamed you were willing to die too. Don't you feel sorry for her?"

"She didn't kill herself."

"She meant to. It's the same thing."

Fumiko was talking about Otoko again. Meanwhile he could hear oil sizzling in a skillet, probably for pork with cabbage. The aroma of fermented bean paste was becoming stronger.

"Your *miso* soup must be getting overdone," Oki remarked.

"All right, all right. I know I can't please you with that precious soup—you've complained about it often enough, ordering different kinds of *miso* from all over the country. . . . To pickle your wife in it, I suppose."

"Do you know how to write the name for that soup in Chinese?"

"Can't you just write it phonetically?"

"You repeat the character for 'honorable' three times."

"Oh?"

"That's because it was always so important in the cuisine, and so tricky to get just right."

"Maybe your honorable *miso* is feeling cross this morning because your precious soup wasn't treated respectfully enough."

She was taunting him again. Oki came from the western part of Japan, and had never really mastered Tokyo polite speech; Fumiko, however, had been brought up in Tokyo, so he often asked her help with it. Yet he did not always accept what she told him. A tenacious argument would turn into an endless squabble, and he would declare that Tokyo speech was only a vulgar dialect with a shallow tradition. In Kyoto or Osaka, he would insist, even ordinary gossip was usually very polite, quite unlike Tokyo gossip. All sorts of things—mountains and rivers, houses, streets, heavenly bodies, even fish and vegetables—were referred to with polite expressions.

"In that case, you'd better ask Taichiro," she would say, dropping the argument. "After all, he's a scholar."

"What would he know about it? He may know something about literature, but he's never studied polite language. Look at the sloppy way he and his friends talk! Even in his articles he can't write proper Japanese."

Actually, Oki disliked either consulting his son or being instructed by him. He preferred to ask his wife. But although Fumiko was a Tokyoite, his questions often left her confused.

Again this morning he found himself complaining about the decay of language.

"In the past, scholars knew their Chinese and could write a correct, well-turned prose."

"People don't talk like that. Funny new words get born every day, like those baby mice, and it doesn't matter to them what they nibble at. Words change so fast it makes your head spin."

"So they have only a short life, and even if they survive they're dated—like the novels we write. It's rare for one to last five years."

"Well, maybe it's enough if a new word lasts overnight." Fumiko brought in the breakfast tray. "I've done well to survive too, all these years since you were thinking of dying with that girl."

"Because there's no retirement age in the housewife business. Too bad."

"But there's divorce. I've wanted to know myself what it feels like to be divorced, at least once in my life."

"It's not too late."

"I don't want to anymore. You know the old saying about trying to seize opportunity by the forelock, after it's fallen out."

"Yours hasn't—you aren't even gray yet."

"But yours has!"

"That's my sacrifice to avoid divorce. So that you won't be jealous."

"You *will* make me angry!"

Bantering as usual, they went on with breakfast. If anything, Fumiko seemed in a good humor. She had thought of Otoko, but this morning she was evidently not in a mood to dig up the past.

The rain had slackened, though as yet there were no rifts in the clouds.

"Is Taichiro still asleep?" Oki asked her. "Get him up!"

Fumiko nodded. "All right, but I doubt if I can. He'll tell me to let him sleep because he's on vacation."

"Isn't he going to Kyoto today?"

"He can leave for the airport after dinner. . . . Why is he going anyway, when it's so hot?"

"Maybe you should ask him. He's taken it into his head to visit Sanetaka's grave again, behind the Nisonin Temple. It seems he's going to write a thesis on the *Sanetaka Chronicle*. . . . Do you know who Sanetaka was?"

"A court noble?"

"Of course he was a noble! He rose to be chamberlain under Yoshimasa, and he was a friend of the poet Sogi and his circle. Sanetaka was one of the aristocrats who

kept literature and art alive during the wars of the sixteenth century. He seems to have had an interesting
personality, and he left an enormous diary. Taichiro
wants to use it to study the culture of that period."

"Oh? And where is the temple?"

"At the foot of Mt. Ogura."

"But where is that? Didn't you take me there once?"

"A long time ago. It was the place with all the poetic
associations."

"That was in Saga, wasn't it? Now I remember."

"Taichiro is dredging up so many incidental details
that he says I should put them into a novel. He calls them
worthless anecdotes. I suppose he thinks he's quite a
scholar, telling me I can liven up a novel with his worthless anecdotes and blown-up legends."

Fumiko smiled discreetly.

"Go wake your young scholar!" Oki got up from the
table. "Who ever heard of a son sleeping while his father
is already at work?"

He went into his study and sat at the desk, head
propped in his hands, reflecting on their exchange about
a retirement age for novelists. It did not seem at all
funny. He heard someone gargling in the lavatory. Taichiro came in wiping his face with a towel.

"A little late, aren't you?" Oki asked sharply.

"I was just lying there daydreaming."

"Daydreaming about what?"

"Father, did you know they excavated the tomb of
Princess Kazunomiya?"

"They violated a princess's grave?"

"I suppose you could call it that," said Taichiro placatingly. "Don't they often excavate old tombs for scholarly research?"

"But if it's Princess Kazunomiya's tomb it couldn't be very old. When did she die, anyway?"

"In 1877," he answered promptly.

"Then it's less than a century ago!"

"That's right. But they say she was just a skeleton."
Oki frowned.

"They say even her pillow and all her clothing had disintegrated—there was nothing but the skeleton."

"It's inhuman to dig up a grave like that."

"She was in a lovely, innocent pose, like a child taking a nap."

"The skeleton?"

"Yes. And it seems there was a hank of hair behind the skull—widow's length, but it was black hair that suggested a highborn woman who died young."

"Were you daydreaming about her?"

"Yes, but there was something else too, something beautiful and mysterious and fragile. . . . "

"What was it?" Oki could not respond to his son's enthusiasm. He felt disgusted by the insolence of digging up the skeleton of a tragic Imperial Princess, who must have died before she was thirty.

"Something you'd never think of." Taichiro stood there dangling his towel. "Why don't I go get Mother and tell her about it too?" Oki nodded.

Taichiro was repeating the story to his mother as he came back with her to the study.

Oki had taken a volume of the *Dictionary of Japanese History* from the bookshelf in the corridor, opened it to the entry on Kazunomiya, and lit a cigarette. His son was holding what looked like a slender magazine. Oki asked if it was the excavation report.

"No, it's a museum journal. One of the staff members wrote an essay called 'Vanishing Beauty' about something ghostlike they saw. Maybe it isn't mentioned in the report." He began summarizing the essay for them. "A glass plate a little larger than a calling card was found between the arms of the skeleton of Princess Kazunomiya. That seems to have been the only thing they found with her. They were excavating the tombs of the Tokugawa Shoguns in Shiba, so they opened Kazunomiya's too. . . . The man in charge of textiles thought it might be a pocket mirror, or a wet-plate photograph. He wrapped it in paper and took it back to the museum."

"Is that a photograph on glass?" his mother asked.

"Yes, you spread an emulsion on a glass plate, and it's developed while it's still wet. Like those old photographs, you know."

"Oh, those."

"The glass looked transparent, but when the textile expert examined it at the museum, holding it to the light at various angles, he could see the figure of a young man wearing ceremonial robes and a court hat. It *was* a photograph. Badly faded, of course."

"Was it the Shogun Iemochi?" Oki asked, becoming interested.

"So it seems. Presumably she was buried holding a photograph of her dead husband. The textile man thought so too, and he was going to consult the Research Institute for Cultural Properties the next day, hoping they could bring it out more clearly somehow or other.

. . . But by morning the image had faded away completely. Overnight the photograph had turned into plain glass."

"Really?" Fumiko looked at him in surprise.

"That's because it was exposed to the air and light after being buried for years," said Oki.

"That's right. There's a witness to prove the textile man saw a real photograph. He showed it to a guard who came around just as he was looking at it, and the guard said he saw the same image of a young nobleman."

"My!"

"The essay calls it 'truly a story of fleeting life.'" Taichiro paused. "But the staff member who wrote it has literary aspirations, so instead of ending there he went on to embellish it. You know Prince Arisugawa was said to be deeply in love with Kazunomiya. Maybe the photograph showed her lover instead of her husband. Maybe when Kazunomiya was dying she secretly ordered her attendants to bury the glass photograph of her lover along with her corpse. That's what one would expect of a tragic princess, he says."

"Just his imagination, don't you think? It makes a good story to have a picture of her lover vanish overnight, after being brought back from the grave."

"He says that the picture should have been buried in the earth forever. Kazunomiya would have wanted it to disappear that night."

"I suppose she would."

"This suddenly vanishing beauty could be recaptured by a writer and made into a moving work of art—that's how he ends his essay. Wouldn't you like to write something about it, Father?"

"I'm not sure I could," said Oki. "Maybe as a short story, beginning with a scene at the excavation. . . . But isn't the essay enough?"

"Do you think so?" He seemed disappointed. "I read it in bed this morning, and had an urge to tell you about it. I'll leave it here for you." He put the journal on his father's desk.

"I'd like to read it."

As Taichiro was going to the door Fumiko asked: "What about the princess's skeleton? They didn't take her off to a college or a museum, did they? That would be *too* cruel! They must have buried her again just as she was, surely."

"The essay doesn't say, but probably they did."

"Still, the picture she was holding is gone—the poor dead princess must be lonely."

"That didn't occur to me," he said. "Father, would you end with a touch like that?"

"It's a bit too sentimental."

Taichiro left the study. Fumiko was about to leave too. "Aren't you planning to work?" she asked.

"Not yet. After a story like that I need a walk." Oki got up from his desk. "It seems to have stopped raining."

"Anyway, it ought to be nice and cool after such a downpour." She glanced out at the cloudy sky. "Please go through the kitchen, and take a look at the leak."

"You talk about how lonely the poor dead princess must be, and in the next breath you tell me to go look at a leak."

His clogs were in the shoe box at the kitchen entrance. As Fumiko took them out for him, she said: "Do you think it's all right for Taichiro to talk about a tomb, and then go visit one in Kyoto?"

Oki was startled. "Why not? You really do jump from one thing to another!"

"I'm not jumping. I've been wondering from the time he began telling us about Princess Kazunomiya."

"But Sanetaka's tomb is hundreds of years older."

"He's going to Kyoto to meet that young lady!"

Again Oki was caught off guard. Fumiko had been squatting to set out his clogs, but now as he slipped into them she stood up and looked him in the eye.

"That frighteningly beautiful young lady—don't you think she's frightening?"

Oki hesitated. He had kept his night with Keiko secret from her.

"I have an uneasy feeling about it." Fumiko's eyes were still on him. "We haven't had a real thunderstorm yet this summer."

"There you go, jumping again!"

"If we have a bad storm tonight, lightning might strike the plane."

"Don't be ridiculous! I've never heard of an airplane being struck by lightning in Japan."

Glad to be safely out of the house, Oki noticed dark rain clouds and a lowering sky. The dampness was oppressive. But even if the sky cleared he would hardly have felt exhilarated. The thought of his son going to Kyoto to see Keiko weighed on his mind. Of course he could not be certain, but ever since his wife had surprised him with the notion it had begun to seem likely.

When he left his study to go for a walk he had intended to visit one of the old Kamakura temples, but because of Fumiko's odd remark the tombs on the temple grounds seemed repellent to him. Instead he went to climb a small wooded hill near his house. The hill was rich with the fragrance of summer trees and earth after the rain. As he felt himself becoming hidden among the leaves, memories of Keiko's lovely body came rising up vividly before him.

First he saw one of her nipples. It was a pink nipple, almost transparently pink. Some Japanese women have fair skin glowing with femininity, perhaps even finer and more lustrous than the faintly pink gleaming skin of young girls in the West. And the nipples of some Japanese girls are an incomparably delicate shade of pink. Keiko's complexion was not quite so fair, but the pink of her nipple seemed freshly washed and moist. It was like a flower bud against her creamy breast. It had no ugly little wrinkles or granular texture, and was just the right modest size to suckle on lovingly.

But it was not only its beauty that brought the image of Keiko's nipple back to Oki. Although she had allowed him her right nipple at the hotel that night, she had avoided giving the left one. When he tried to touch it, she pressed down hard on it with the palm of her hand. And when he pulled her hand away, Keiko turned and twisted, recoiling from him.

"Don't do that! Please! . . . The left one is no good."

Oki's hand froze. "What's wrong with it?"

"It doesn't come out."

"Doesn't come out?" He was bewildered.

"It's no good. I hate it." Keiko was still breathing in gasps. Oki could not understand.

What was it that did not "come out"? What was "no good"? Could it be that her left nipple was sunken, or misshapen? Was Keiko worried about being deformed? Or was she a shy young girl who could not bear to reveal that her nipples did not match? He recalled that when he picked her up in his arms and put her on the bed, and she curled herself into a ball, she seemed to protect her left breast more than the other one, pressing it tightly under the crook of her left arm. However, he had seen both of her breasts, before as well as after that. Anything odd about the form of her left nipple ought to have attracted his attention.

In fact, even when he forcibly pulled Keiko's hand away and looked at the left nipple, he saw nothing unnatural about it. Examining it closely, all he could tell was that the left one might be a trifle smaller than the right. That was not unusual—why should Keiko be so anxious to keep it from him?

Her resistance made him all the more eager. Vigorously seeking out her left nipple, he said: "Is there some one special person you let touch it?"

Keiko shook her head. "No. There's no one." She stared up at him wide-eyed. He could not be sure, but her eyes seemed sad, almost tearful. At least it was not the look of a woman being caressed. Although Keiko closed her eyes again and let him do as he pleased, she seemed withdrawn. Oki noticed and relaxed his grip, but then she began undulating as if that excited her all the more.

Was Keiko's right breast a somewhat spoiled virgin, and the left still virginal? Oki realized that they gave her different feelings. He could understand why she might say the left one was "no good." That would be extremely bold, for a girl being caressed by him for the first time. Possibly it was the tactic of an extraordinarily guileful young girl. Any man would be tempted by the thought of a woman deriving a different level of pleasure from her two breasts, and would want to try to equalize them. Even if she had been born that way, and nothing could be done, the very abnormality would tempt him. Oki had never known a woman whose nipples were so different in their sensitivity.

To be sure, all women differed more or less in the ways

they liked to be caressed. Was Keiko's reaction merely a striking instance of this? Indeed, many women had had their tastes cultivated by the habits of their lovers. In that case, an insensitive left nipple would be an especially tempting target—probably the difference had been created by someone inexperienced with women. The thought that the left one was still a virgin whetted his appetite. But to equalize them would take time. He was not sure he could meet her so often.

Hence it was foolish to seek out her left nipple against her wish, when he was embracing her for the first time. He began to search instead for the places where she liked to be caressed. He found them. And then, just as he was beginning to handle her more roughly, he heard her call out to Otoko. He flinched, and Keiko pushed him away. She sat up in bed, and then got up and went to the dressing table to brush her tangled hair. He did not want to look.

As the rain became heavy again, he was plunged into a lonely mood. Loneliness seemed to come and go as it pleased.

Keiko returned and knelt beside the bed. "Will you put your arms around me and go to sleep now?" she said coaxingly, peering into his face.

Without a word Oki put his left arm around her and stretched out on his back. Keiko joined him and snuggled close. Memories of Otoko came to him one after another. After a while he broke the silence: "Now I notice your scent."

"My scent?"

"The smell of a woman."

"Oh? Because it's so hot and sticky. . . . I'm sorry."

"No, it's not that. The good smell of a woman."

It was the scent that comes naturally from a woman's skin when she lies in the embrace of a lover. Any woman would have it, even a young girl. It not only arouses a man but reassures and gratifies him. The woman's willingness to yield herself seems to emanate from her whole body.

Oki had nestled his face between her breasts to let her know that it was a good smell. He had lain there quietly with his eyes closed, enveloped in her scent.

Even now, here in the grove, the last image of her body to come rising up before him was that of her nipple. It was as fresh and vivid as ever.

I mustn't let Taichiro see her, he told himself. I mustn't let him.

He was holding the trunk of a slender tree in a tight grip.

But what can I do? He shook the tree, dislodging a shower of raindrops. The ground was still so wet that his clogs were soaked at the toe. Oki gazed at the green leaves surrounding him. All at once he felt smothered by that dense cover of green.

There seemed to be only one way to keep his son from seeing Keiko: telling him that he had spent the night with her at Enoshima. Otherwise, perhaps he could try sending a telegram to Otoko, or directly to Keiko.

Oki hurried home and asked for Taichiro.

"He's gone to Tokyo," his wife said.

"Already? But he's taking an evening plane. Do you think he'll come home again first?"

"No. That would be out of his way. . . . He said he wanted to stop in at school to pick up some research materials."

"I wonder."

"Is anything wrong? You're not looking well."

Avoiding her eyes, Oki went into his study. He had missed Taichiro and had not sent a telegram to Otoko or Keiko.

Taichiro flew to Kyoto by the six o'clock plane. Keiko was waiting at the airport.

He fumbled for a greeting. "You shouldn't have—I had no idea you'd come out to meet me."

"Aren't you grateful?"

"I am. But you shouldn't have bothered." She saw that his eyes were alight, and lowered her gaze demurely.

"Did you come from Kyoto?" he asked, still rather ill at ease.

"Yes, from Kyoto," Keiko replied politely. "I live there, after all. Where else would I be coming from?"

He started to laugh apologetically and looked down, his eyes resting on her obi. "You're so dazzling, it's hard to believe you're here to meet someone like me."

"My kimono?"

"Yes, your kimono, and your obi, and . . . " Your hair and your face too, he wanted to say.

"In the summer I feel cooler if I wear a proper kimono, with the obi snug. I don't like loose-fitting clothing when it's hot."

Still, her kimono and obi seemed brand-new. "I prefer quiet colors for summer, like this obi," she said. "I painted the design myself." She was following close behind him as he made his way toward the baggage area.

Taichiro turned to look.

"What do you think it is?" she asked.

"Let's see—water? A stream?"

"It's a rainbow! A colorless rainbow . . . just curved lines in light and dark ink. Nobody would recognize it, but I'm supposed to be wrapped in a summer rainbow—in the mountains at dusk." Turning, Keiko displayed the back of her silk organdy obi. On its puffed-out bow there were green mountain ranges, and the delicate rose-colored shading of a sunset sky.

"The two sides don't match," she went on, keeping her back toward him. "An odd girl painted it, so it's an odd obi." He was captivated by the combination of the faint flush of rose with the creamy skin at the nape of her slender neck under her upswept black hair.

Passengers for Kyoto were provided with taxi service to the airline office. The first taxi quickly filled, but while Taichiro was wondering what to do another came up, and he was able to ride alone with Keiko. As they were leaving the airport, he remarked: "You must not have had dinner yet, coming all the way out to meet me at this hour."

"And you're still treating me like a stranger! . . . I

didn't even want lunch—I'll have something later, with you." Then she said softly: "You know, I was watching you from the time you left the door of the plane. You were the seventh one out."

"Was I?"

"The seventh," Keiko repeated distinctly. "You didn't even look around for me as you came down the steps. If you expect someone to meet you, isn't it natural to see who is at the gate? But you just kept walking along looking down. It made me so ashamed I wanted to hide."

"I didn't expect you."

"Then why did you write special delivery to tell me when you'd arrive?"

"I suppose I wanted you to know I was really coming."

"It was like a telegram—nothing but the time of your plane! I wondered if you were testing me, to see if I'd come. Weren't you testing me? Anyway, I came."

"But I'd have looked to see if you were there, wouldn't I?"

"You didn't say where you'd be staying either. If I hadn't come to the airport, how would I have known?"

"Well . . . " Taichiro hesitated. "I just wanted to tell you I was coming to Kyoto."

"I don't like it. I don't know what you were trying to do!"

"I thought I might phone you."

"And if you didn't, would you go on home to Kamakura? Did you only want me to know you were here? Were you trying to humiliate me, being in Kyoto and not seeing me?"

"No, I wrote so that I'd have the courage to see you."

"The courage to see me?" Her voice sank to a whisper. "Can I be happy? Or must I be sad? Never mind, don't answer—I'm glad I came! But I'm not a girl you have to have courage to see. Sometimes I want to die. Go ahead and trample on me!"

"Why are you bursting out like that, all of a sudden?"

"It's *not* sudden. That's the kind of girl I am. I need somebody to destroy my pride."

"I'm afraid I'm not the sort to hurt anyone's pride."

"So it seems, but that won't do. You can walk all over me!"

"Why do you say such things?"

"I don't know." Keiko pressed her hand lightly against her hair, in the rush of wind through the car window. "Maybe I'm unhappy. . . . Just now when you were coming to the gate you looked downcast and gloomy. Why were you so sad? I was waiting to meet you, but I didn't exist for you, did I?"

The fact was that he had been thinking of her, but he could not admit it.

"Even that made me unhappy. Because I'm selfish. . . . How can I get you to think I exist?"

"I'm always thinking of you," he declared. "At this moment, too."

"Are you?" Keiko murmured. "It's strange to be here beside you. I just want to sit and listen to you talk."

Their taxi passed the new factories at Ibaraki and Takatsuki. In the hills near Yamazaki the illuminated Suntory Distillery loomed up before them.

"Wasn't your flight bumpy?" she asked. "I worried about you—there was a heavy afternoon shower in Kyoto."

"It was smooth enough, but once I thought we were going to crash. We were flying straight into some dark mountains that blocked our way."

Keiko's hand came stealing over.

"They turned out to be black clouds," he said. His hand lay still under her palm. She kept her hand on his for a time.

The taxi entered Kyoto and headed east on Fifth Street. No breeze stirred the trailing branches of the willows along the broad street, but the shower seemed to have cooled the air. Far at the end of the green rows of willows were the Eastern Hills. The line of hills was blurred by low-hanging clouds in the evening sky. Here at the western edge of the city he could already feel the atmosphere of Kyoto.

They went up Horikawa, and then along Oike Street to the JAL office.

Taichiro had reserved a room at the Kyoto Hotel and said he wanted to leave his suitcase there. "Let's walk over. It's just down the block."

"No, no! I don't want to!" Keiko shook her head. She got back into the waiting taxi and beckoned to him. "Kiyamachi above Third Street," she told the driver.

"Stop at the Kyoto Hotel on the way," Taichiro added. But Keiko objected.

"Never mind," she said. "Please go straight to Kiyamachi."

They arrived at a tea house with a narrow alleyway entrance that he found intriguing, and were shown into a little room overlooking the river. He was delighted by the view and asked how she happened to know a place like this.

"My teacher often comes here."

"You mean Miss Ueno?" He turned toward her.

"Yes, Miss Ueno." Then she left the room. Is she going to order dinner? he wondered. About five minutes later Keiko came back and said: "If you don't mind, I'd like you to stay here. I just called to cancel your other reservation."

Taichiro stared at her in amazement. She was looking down meekly. "I'm sorry. I wanted you somewhere I knew."

He was at a loss for words.

"Please, stay here. You'll only be in Kyoto two or three days, won't you?"

"Yes."

Keiko glanced up at him. Her unpainted, beautifully even eyebrows seemed a shade lighter than her lashes, and gave a look of innocence to her jet-black eyes. She had used only a touch of pale lipstick but her lips were exquisitely shaped. She did not appear to be wearing any rouge or powder.

"Stop it!" she said, blinking. "Why are you looking at me like that?"

"You have such thick lashes."

"They're real! Pull them and see."

"I do feel like giving them a tug."

"Go ahead, I don't mind." She shut her eyes and held her face closer. "Maybe they seem so long because they're curled."

Keiko waited, but Taichiro did not touch her eyelashes. "Open your eyes," he said. "Look up a little, and open your eyes wide." She did as he asked.

"Do you want me to look straight at you?"

Just then a waitress brought in drinks and appetizers.

"Would you like sake or beer?" said Keiko, settling back. "I don't drink, myself."

The paper screens to the balcony were almost closed, and a lively party, with geisha, seemed to be going on out there. A hush fell over the party as the wail of a Chinese fiddle and the songs of strolling musicians drifted up from the promenade by the river.

"What are your plans for tomorrow?" Keiko asked.

"First I want to visit a tomb on the hill behind the Nisonin Temple. It's a nice one, an old court-family tomb."

"I can go along with you, can't I?" She was looking toward the electric fan. "I'd like you to take me for a motorboat ride on Lake Biwa. It doesn't have to be to-morrow."

Taichiro was hesitant. "I don't know how to handle a motorboat."

"I do."

"Can you swim?"

"In case it turns over?" she said, looking at him. "You can rescue me! You will, won't you? I'll hang on to you."

"I couldn't rescue you if you did."

"What *should* I do?"

"I'd have to hold you up, with my arms around you from behind." Suddenly he felt embarrassed, imagining himself trying to keep this beautiful girl afloat. . . . Unless he held her tight both of their lives would be in danger.

"I don't care if it turns over," said Keiko.

"I'm not sure I could rescue you."

"What if you couldn't?"

"Don't talk like that! Let's give up the motorboat ride."

"But I've been looking forward to it. There's nothing to worry about." She poured some more beer into his glass. "Aren't you going to change into a kimono?"

"No, I'm all right."

Two night kimonos—a man's and a woman's—were lying neatly folded in a corner. Taichiro tried not to look at them. Had Keiko reserved a room for two?

There was no adjoining room. He could not bring himself to change in front of her.

The waitress brought in their dinner without a word. Keiko was silent too.

They began to hear the twang of a samisen coming from a balcony down the river. The party on their own balcony was getting noisy; loud Osaka voices were plainly audible. The sentimental songs and the sound of the Chinese fiddle were fading into the distance.

The river could not be seen from where they were sitting, at the low table in the middle of the room.

"Does he know you've come to Kyoto?" Keiko asked.

"My father? Yes, of course. But he'd never guess you met me at the airport, and I'm here with you."

"That makes me happy! Having you slip away from your father to be with me."

"I'm not trying to hide anything from him. . . . Is that how it seems to you?"

"But that's how it *is*!"

"And your Miss Ueno?"

"I haven't breathed a word to her. Still, I wouldn't be surprised if both of them had an inkling of it. That would *really* make me happy."

"It's not very likely. Miss Ueno hasn't heard about us, has she? Did you say anything to her?"

"I told her you showed me around Kamakura. When I said I liked you she turned pale!" Keiko's black eyes gleamed, and her cheeks flushed slightly. "Do you think she could be indifferent to the child of a man who caused her so much suffering? She told me how she felt when your sister was born."

Taichiro was silent.

"Miss Ueno is working on a picture she calls *Ascension of an Infant*. It's a baby sitting on a five-colored cloud— though it seems her own baby died before she was able to sit up." Keiko paused. "If that child had lived she'd be older than your sister."

"Why are you telling me all this?"

"I wanted to get revenge for Miss Ueno."

"Revenge on my father?"

"And on you too!"

Taichiro was prying clumsily at the broiled sweetfish

before him. Keiko drew his dish over and expertly boned the fish. "Has your father said anything about me?" she asked.

"No. I don't talk to him about you."

"Why not?"

His face clouded. He felt as if a cold hand had touched him.

"I've never talked to my father about women," he blurted out.

"About *women*?" An enchanting smile came to her lips.

"How did you intend to get revenge on me?" he asked in a dry voice.

"I can't say, really. . . . Perhaps it was by falling in love with you." Her eyes had a faraway look, as if she were gazing across the river. "Don't you think that's funny?"

"So falling in love is your revenge?"

Keiko nodded meekly, as if relieved. "It's feminine jealousy," she murmured.

"Jealousy over what?"

"I'm jealous because Miss Ueno still loves your father . . . because she doesn't bear the least grudge toward him."

"Do you love her that much?"

"Enough to die for her."

"I can't help what happened in the distant past. But does our being here together have anything to do with that old tie between Miss Ueno and my father?"

"Of course. If I weren't living with her you wouldn't exist for me. I'd never even have met you."

"You shouldn't think such thoughts. A young girl who thinks like that is haunted by the ghosts of the past. Maybe that's why your neck is so slender and wraithlike. Beautifully slender, of course."

"A slender neck means you've never loved a man—that's what Miss Ueno says. But I'd hate for it to be thick."

He suppressed the temptation to grasp that beautiful neck. "That's the whispering of a ghost. You're caught in a spell, Keiko."

"No—in love!"

"Miss Ueno doesn't really know anything about me, does she?"

"When I came back from Kamakura I told her you must be the image of your father when he was your age."

"That's ridiculous!" Taichiro said hotly. "I don't look at all like my father."

"Does that make you angry? You'd rather not look like him?"

"You've been trying to deceive me ever since you met me at the airport, haven't you? You don't want me to know *what* you think."

"I'm not trying to deceive you."

"Then that's the way you always talk?"

"You're being awfully unfair."

"You said I could walk all over you, you know."

"And you have to do that to get me to tell the truth? I'm not lying—you simply refuse to understand me! Aren't *you* the one who's hiding your thoughts? That's why I'm unhappy."

"Are you?"

"Of course I am. I don't know whether I'm happy or not!"

"I don't know why I'm here with you, either."

"Isn't it because you love me?"

"Yes, but . . . "

"But what?"

Taichiro did not answer.

"But what?" Keiko pressed his hand between her palms and shook it.

"You're not eating," he said. She had hardly touched her dinner.

"The bride doesn't eat at the wedding reception."

"There, that's the kind of thing you say."

"You're the one who started talking about food!"

SUMMER
LOSSES

Otoko was the sort of person who lost weight in summer.

When she was a girl in Tokyo she never worried about it; only in her early twenties, after living in Kyoto for some years, had she clearly realized her tendency to become thinner during the hot weather. Her mother pointed it out to her.

"You seem to waste away in the summer too, don't you, Otoko?" her mother had said. "Something you inherited from me—it's finally come out. We have the same kind of weaknesses. I've always thought you were strong-minded, but physically you're my own child. There's no arguing about it."

"I'm not at all strong-minded."

"You have a violent disposition."

"I'm *not* violent!"

No doubt her mother was thinking of Otoko's love

affair with Oki when she called her strong-minded. But was that not a young girl's ardor, a frantic intensity of feeling quite apart from weakness or strength of will?

They had come to Kyoto because Otoko's mother wanted to distract her daughter from her sorrow, and so they both avoided mentioning Oki's name. However, being alone together in an unfamiliar city, with only one another to turn to for consolation, they could not help glimpsing the Oki in each other's heart. For the mother, her daughter seemed to be a mirror reflecting Oki, and for the daughter her mother was another such mirror. And each saw her own reflection in the other's mirror.

One day while writing a letter Otoko happened to open the dictionary to the character for "think." As she scanned its other meanings ("yearn for," "be unable to forget," "be sad") she felt her chest tighten. She was afraid to touch the dictionary—Oki was even there. Innumerable words reminded her of him. To link whatever she saw and heard with her love was nothing less than to be alive. Her awareness of her body was inseparable from her memory of his embrace.

Otoko understood very well that her mother—a lone woman with an only child—was anxious for her to forget him. But she did not want to forget. She seemed to cling to his memory as if she could not live without it. Probably she had been able to leave the barred room in the psychiatric ward because of her steadfast love for Oki.

Once when he was making love to her, Otoko moaned deliriously and begged him to stop. Oki loosed his hold, and she opened her eyes. The pupils were dilated and glistening. "I can hardly see you, Sonny-boy. Your face looks blurred, as if it's under a stream." Even at such a moment she called him "Sonny-boy."

"You know, if you died I couldn't go on living. I simply couldn't!" Tears glinted in the corners of Otoko's eyes. They were not tears of sadness but of surrender.

"Then there'd be no one like you to remember me," said Oki.

"I couldn't bear just remembering the man I love. I'd rather die too. You'd let me, wouldn't you?" Otoko nudged her face against his throat.

At first he did not take her seriously. Then he said: "I suppose if anyone pulled a knife on me, or threatened me with a pistol, you'd step forward to protect me."

"I'd gladly give my life for yours, anytime."

"That's not what I meant. But if some danger loomed up before me you'd throw yourself forward to shield me, without even thinking, wouldn't you?"

"Of course."

"No man would do that for me. Only this little girl——"

"I'm not little!" said Otoko.

"Are you really so grown-up?" he asked, fondling her breasts.

Oki was also thinking of the unborn child that she was carrying, and of what might become of it if he were suddenly to die. That was something Otoko learned later, when she read his novel.

When her mother had remarked that Otoko seemed to waste away in the summer, perhaps she was also thinking that by now her daughter was surely not losing weight because of memories of Oki.

Although Otoko was delicately built, with fine bones and sloping shoulders, she had never been seriously ill. Of course she became worn and thin, with a strange look in her eye, after all the troubles caused by her love affair. But she soon recovered physically. The youthful resilience of her body made her still wounded feelings seem incongruous. Except for her melancholy look when she thought of Oki, no one would have been aware of her sadness. Even that occasional shadow, the expression of a young girl's yearning, only enhanced her beauty.

Otoko had known since childhood that her mother lost weight in summer. She often wiped the perspiration from her mother's back and chest, and knew very well, though she did not mention it, that her thinness came from susceptibility to the heat. But Otoko was too young to worry about having inherited that weakness, until she heard it from her mother. She must have had a tendency to it for years.

From her mid-twenties Otoko always wore a kimono, and so her slenderness was not as obvious as it would have been in skirts or slacks. Still, there was no denying how thin she became every summer. In later years it reminded her of her dead mother.

Summer by summer, Otoko's weakness and loss of weight seemed more severe.

"What kind of tonic is good for this?" she once asked her mother. "There are lots of medicines advertised in the papers—have you tried any of them?"

"Well, they must do some good," her mother answered vaguely. After a pause, she went on in a different tone: "Otoko, the best medicine for a woman is getting married."

Otoko was silent.

"A man is the kind of medicine that gives a woman life! All women have to take it."

"Even if it's poison?"

"Even then. You took poison once, and you still don't realize it, do you? But I know you can find a good antidote. Sometimes you need a poison to counteract a poison. Maybe the medicine is bitter, but you have to shut your eyes and swallow it. You may even gag, and think it won't go down your throat."

Otoko's mother died without having seen her daughter follow her advice. No doubt that was her last regret. It was true that Otoko had never thought of Oki as a poison. Even in the room with the barred windows she felt no resentment or hatred toward him. It was only that she was half-crazed with love. The powerful drug she took to kill herself was soon completely purged from her body; Oki and his baby were gone from her too, and the scars they left might have been expected to fade. Yet her love for Oki remained undiminished.

Time passed. But time flows in many streams. Like a river, an inner stream of time will flow rapidly at some places and sluggishly at others, or perhaps even stand hopelessly stagnant. Cosmic time is the same for everyone, but human time differs with each person. Time flows in the same way for all human beings; every human being flows through time in a different way.

As Otoko approached forty she wondered if the fact that Oki remained within her meant that this stream of time was stagnant, rather than flowing. Or had her image of him flowed along with her through time, like a flower drifting down a river? How she drifted along in his stream of time she did not know. Although he could not have forgotten her, time would at least have flowed differently for him. Even if two people were lovers, their streams of time would never be the same. . . .

Today too, as she had been doing every morning when she awakened, Otoko massaged her forehead with her fingertips, and then ran her hands over the back of her neck and under her arms. Her skin was damp. She felt as if the dampness oozing from her pores had soaked into her night kimono.

Keiko seemed to be attracted by the odor and the sleekness of Otoko's damp skin, and sometimes wanted to peel off whatever she wore next to her body. Otoko hated intensely to smell of perspiration.

Last night, though, Keiko had come home after twelve-thirty, and had sat down uneasily, avoiding Otoko's eyes.

Otoko was lying in bed, shielding her face from the ceiling light with a round fan and gazing at the half dozen sketches of a baby's face that were tacked on the wall. She seemed absorbed in them, and merely glanced over at Keiko. "Late, aren't you?"

Otoko had not been allowed to see her premature

baby, but was told that it had had jet-black hair. When she wanted to know more about the baby her mother had said: "She was a sweet little thing, and looked just like you." That was only to console her, Otoko felt. In recent years she had seen photographs of newborn babies, but they all seemed ugly. There was even an occasional photograph of a baby being delivered, or still attached to its mother by the umbilical cord, but these she found quite repulsive.

Thus she had no idea of the face and form of her baby, only a vision in her heart. She knew very well that the child in her *Ascension of an Infant* would not look like her dead baby, and she had no wish to paint a realistic portrait. What she wanted was to express her sense of loss, her grief and affection for someone she had never seen. She had cherished that desire so long that the image of the dead infant had become a symbol of yearning to her. She thought of it whenever she felt sad. Also the picture was to symbolize herself surviving all these years, as well as the beauty and sadness of her love for Oki.

Otoko had not yet succeeded in painting an infant's face that satisfied her. The holy faces of cherubs and of the Christ child were usually firmly outlined, either artificial-looking or like miniature adults. Rather than such a strong, clear-cut face, she wanted to portray a faint, dreamlike one, a haloed spirit neither of this world nor of the world beyond. It should convey a gentle, soothing feeling, and yet also suggest a brimming pool of sorrow. Still, she did not want it to be too abstract.

And how was she to paint the wizened body of a premature baby? How should she treat the background, the minor motifs? Again Otoko looked through her albums of Redon and Chagall, but these delicate fantasies were too alien to stimulate her own imagination.

Once more the old Japanese portraits of a saintly child came before her eyes: portraits based on the legend of the youthful Saint Kobo dreaming that he sat on an eight-petaled lotus talking with the Buddha. In the oldest of them the figure seemed pure and austere, but later it softened and took on a voluptuous charm, until there were even "boys" that could be mistaken for beautiful little girls.

On the night before the Festival of the Full Moon, when Keiko asked to have her portrait painted, Otoko had suspected that it was her own deep concern for the *Ascension of an Infant* that made her think of doing a classical *Holy Virgin* in the manner of the portraits of the boy saint. But afterward she began to wonder if her attraction to the portraits of Saint Kobo might not have an element of self-love, of infatuation with herself. Perhaps in both cases she had a hidden desire for a self-portrait. Might not these sacred visions be nothing other than a vision of a saintly Otoko? The doubt stabbed like a sword, plunged by herself against her will into her own breast. She had to draw it out. But the scar remained, and at times it hurt.

Of course Otoko had no intention of copying the portraits of the boy saint. Yet obviously that image was lurking in the depths of her heart. Even the titles *Ascension of an Infant* and *Holy Virgin* suggested that through these pictures she wanted to purify, indeed to sanctify, her love for her dead baby and for Keiko.

Keiko had taken the youthful portrait of Otoko's mother for a self-portrait when she first saw it. After that the picture always reminded Otoko that Keiko, besides mistaking the woman in the picture for her had said how lovely she looked. It was out of longing that Otoko had painted her mother as young and beautiful, but perhaps there was an element of self-love there as well. Their natural resemblance could hardly account for it. Perhaps she was actually portraying herself.

Otoko still loved Oki, her baby, and her mother, but could these loves have gone unchanged from the time when they were a tangible reality to her? Could not something of these very loves have been subtly transformed into self-love? Of course she would not be aware of it. She had been parted from her baby and her mother by death, and from Oki by a final separation, and these three still lived within her. Yet Otoko alone gave them this life. Her image of Oki flowed along with her through time, and perhaps her memories of their love affair had been dyed by the color of her love for herself, had even been transformed. It had never occurred to her that bygone memories are merely phantoms and apparitions. Perhaps it was to be expected that a woman who had lived alone for two decades without love or marriage should indulge herself in memories of a sad love, and that her indulgence should take on the color of self-love.

Even if she had been led into her infatuation with her

pupil Keiko, so much younger and of her own sex, was that not another form of infatuation with herself? Otherwise, she would surely never dream of portraying a girl like Keiko—a girl who seemed to be turning predatory, and who had asked to pose in the nude for her—as a Buddhist Holy Virgin sitting on a lotus flower. Had Otoko not wanted to create a pure, lovely image of herself? Apparently the girl of sixteen who loved Oki would always exist within her, never to grow up. Yet she had been unaware of it. . . .

Otoko was extremely fastidious, and on a morning like this, when the sticky heat of a Kyoto summer night had left her kimono damp with perspiration, she would normally have got out of bed as soon as she awakened. But instead she lay there with her head turned toward the wall, looking again at her sketches of a baby. She had had difficulty with them. Although her own baby had lived in this world for a brief time, Otoko wanted to paint a kind of spirit child, a child who had never entered the world of human beings.

Keiko was still sound asleep, her back turned to Otoko. The top of a thin summer linen coverlet was wrapped tightly around her body but had worked down below her breast. She lay on her side, legs together, both feet sticking out below the coverlet. Since Keiko usually dressed in Japanese style, her naturally slim, straight toes had seldom been cramped into high-heeled shoes. Her toes were so fine-boned and slender that Otoko felt as if they belonged to a different sort of being, not quite human. She had come to avoid looking at them. But when she grasped Keiko's toes in her hand she took a curious pleasure in the thought that they could hardly belong to a woman of her own generation. It was an eerie feeling.

A scent of perfume wafted to her. It seemed too rich a fragrance for a young girl, but Otoko recognized it as one that Keiko wore occasionally. She began to wonder why she had worn it last night.

When Keiko came home after midnight Otoko had been too engrossed in gazing at the sketches to pay any particular attention. Keiko hurried to bed without even bathing and promptly fell asleep. But perhaps Otoko thought Keiko was sleeping because she herself had soon dropped off to sleep.

As soon as Otoko got up she went around to the other side of Keiko's bed, glanced down at her sleeping face in the dim light, and then began opening the wooden shutters. Keiko was always cheerful in the morning, and would jump up to help the moment she heard Otoko sliding back the shutters. But this morning she only sat up in bed and watched. Finally she rose, and said: "I'm sorry. It must have been almost three before I could get to sleep." She started to take up Otoko's bedding.

"Did the heat bother you?"

"Mmm."

"Don't put away my night kimono, please. I'd like to launder it."

With the kimono over her arm, Otoko went in to bathe. Keiko came along to use the wash basin but seemed to be hurrying even as she brushed her teeth.

"Don't you want to take a bath too?"

"Yes."

"Apparently you went to bed still wearing yesterday's perfume."

"Did I?"

"Indeed you did!" Otoko was suspicious of her vacant air. "Keiko, where were you last night?"

There was no reply.

"Do take a bath. You'll feel better."

"Yes, later on."

"Later?" Otoko looked at her.

By the time Otoko came out of the bathroom Keiko was selecting a kimono from the chest of drawers.

"Are you going out?" Otoko asked sharply.

"Yes."

"You've promised to meet someone?"

"Yes."

"Who is it?"

"Taichiro."

Otoko did not understand.

"Mr. Oki's Taichiro," Keiko explained without hesitation, but omitting "son."

Otoko's voice failed.

"I went to meet him at the airport yesterday, and today I've promised to show him around the city. Or maybe he'll show me around. . . . Otoko, I never hide things from you! First we're going to the Nisonin Temple—he wants to see a tomb on the hill there."

"To see a tomb?" Otoko echoed faintly.

"He says it's the tomb of an old court noble."

"Oh?"

Keiko slipped off her night kimono and stood with her naked back to Otoko. "I think I'll wear a full under-kimono after all. It looks as if it'll be hot again today, but I wouldn't feel right without it."

Silently Otoko watched her dress.

"Now to get the obi nice and tight." Keiko put her hands behind her back and gave a tug.

Otoko looked at Keiko's face in the mirror as she applied some makeup, and Keiko noticed Otoko's reflection too. "Don't stare at me like that."

Otoko tried to soften her expression.

Peering into a wing of the dressing table mirror, Keiko toyed with a lock of hair over one of her beautifully shaped ears, as a finishing touch. Then she started to rise, but sat down again and picked up a bottle of perfume.

Otoko frowned. "Isn't last night's perfume enough?"

"Don't worry."

"Rather fidgety, aren't you?" She paused. "Keiko, why are you seeing him?"

"He wrote to let me know he was coming." She got up, went over to the chest of drawers, and hastily put away several extra kimonos she had taken out in making her selection.

"Fold them neatly," Otoko told her.

"All right."

"You'll have to fold them again."

"All right." But Keiko did not look back at the chest.

"Come over here, please," said Otoko sternly. Keiko

came and sat down with her, looking straight into her eyes. Otoko glanced away, and suddenly asked: "Are you leaving without breakfast?"

"It doesn't matter. I had a late dinner last night."

"As late as all that?"

"Yes."

"Keiko," Otoko began again, "why are you meeting him?"

"I don't know."

"Do you want to?"

"Yes."

"So you're the one who wanted to meet." That seemed clear enough from Keiko's uneasiness. "May I ask why?"

Keiko did not answer.

"Must you see him?" Otoko looked down at her lap. "I'd rather you didn't. Please don't go."

"Why not? It has nothing to do with you, has it?"

"Certainly it has!"

"But you don't even know him."

"You've spent a night with his father, and yet you don't mind seeing him?" Otoko could not bring herself to utter the names "Oki" and "Taichiro."

"Mr. Oki is your old lover, but you've never met Taichiro. He has no connection with you. It's just that he's Mr. Oki's son—he isn't your child."

The words stung Otoko. They reminded her that Oki's wife had given birth to a daughter shortly after her own baby died. "Keiko," she said, "you're seducing him, aren't you?"

"He wrote *me* that he was coming."

"Are you on such good terms with him?"

"I don't like your choice of words."

"What should I say? That you're involved with him?" Otoko wiped her damp forehead with the back of her hand. "You're a fearful person."

There was an odd gleam in Keiko's eye. "Otoko, I hate men."

"Don't go. Please don't. If you do, you needn't come back! If you go out today, you needn't ever come here again!"

"Otoko!" Keiko began to look tearful.

"What are you going to do to Taichiro?" Otoko's hands were trembling in her lap. It was the first time she had spoken his name.

Keiko stood up. "I'm leaving," she said.

"Please don't go."

"Hit me, Otoko. Hit me the way you did the day we went to the Moss Temple." She stood there for a moment as if expecting a blow and then hurried out.

Otoko was bathed in a cold sweat. She sat looking out at the garden, her eyes fixed on the leaves of the square bamboo glistening in the morning sunlight. At last she got up and went into the bathroom. The rush of water startled her—perhaps she had turned it on too hard. Hastily she shut off the faucet, and then turned the water on again to a thin stream and began washing. She felt somewhat calmer, but there was a lingering tension in her head. She pressed a wet towel to her forehead and the back of her neck.

Returning to the other room, Otoko sat down facing her mother's portrait and the sketches of her baby. A shudder of self-loathing passed over her. That came from living with Keiko, but it affected her whole existence, draining her strength and making her utterly wretched. What had she lived for, why was she still alive?

Otoko felt like calling out to her mother. Then she happened to think of Nakamura Tsuné's *Portrait of His Aged Mother,* his last work before preceding her in death. Otoko found it deeply moving, in part because this final painting was of his mother. She had never seen the original, so it was hard to tell what it was really like, but even a photograph of it stirred her emotions.

The young Nakamura Tsuné had painted powerful, sensuous pictures of the woman he loved. He used a great deal of red and was said to have been influenced by Rouault. His *Portrait of Eroshenko,* one of his masterpieces, was a quiet, reverent expression of the noble melancholy of the blind poet, but in warm, lovely colors. However, in that last *Portrait of His Aged Mother* the colors were dark and cold, and his style was very simple. One saw a stooped, emaciated old woman seated in profile against the background of a half-wainscoted wall. A water pitcher stood in a niche in the wall just before her head, and a thermometer was hanging on the other side of her. Of course the thermometer might have been merely added for the sake of the composition, but Otoko was much impressed by it, as well as by the prayer beads dangling from the old woman's fingers, which were resting on her lap. Somehow they seemed to symbolize the feelings of the artist—himself on the verge of dying— toward death. So did the picture as a whole.

Otoko brought an album of Nakamura's paintings from the closet, and compared his portrait of his mother with her own. She had chosen to make a youthful portrait even though her mother had already died. Also, it was by no means her last work, nor was there a shadow of death cast over it. Hers was in an entirely different style, traditionally Japanese, and yet with the reproduction of Nakamura's portrait before her she realized the sentimentality of her own painting. She shut her eyes, forcing her eyelids tight, and felt herself going faint.

Otoko had painted her mother out of a fervent desire for consolation. She had thought of her only as young and beautiful. How shallow and self-indulgent that seemed, compared with the fervent devotion of an artist who was himself near death! Had not her life itself been like that?

She had begun her portrait by sketching from an early photograph of her mother, even showing her as younger and more beautiful than she was then. As she worked, Otoko had occasionally looked at her own face in the mirror, since she resembled her mother. Perhaps it was natural that the picture would have a kind of sweet prettiness—still, could one not also detect the lack of any profound inner spirit?

Otoko recalled that her mother had never allowed herself to be photographed after they came to Kyoto. The magazine photographer from Tokyo had wanted a picture of them together, but her mother had fled—because of her grief, Otoko now suspected. She was living in Kyoto with her daughter like an outcast hiding in shame, and had even cut her ties with friends in Tokyo. Otoko too was not without the feelings of an outcast, but since she was only sixteen when she came to Kyoto her loneliness and isolation were different from her mother's. She was also different in continuing her love for Oki, however wounded by it.

As she studied her portrait, and then Nakamura's, she wondered if she should paint her mother again.

Keiko had gone to meet Oki Taichiro and Otoko felt that she was losing her. She could not suppress her anxiety.

This morning Keiko had not once mentioned "revenge." She said she hated men, but that was nothing to rely on. She had already betrayed herself by leaving without breakfast, on the pretext of a late dinner the night before. What was Keiko going to do to Oki's son? What would become of them, and what should she herself do, after all these years as a captive of her love for Oki? Otoko felt that she could not sit and wait.

Having failed to stop Keiko from leaving, all she could do now was try to pursue her and talk to Taichiro herself. But Keiko had not said where he was staying, or where they were to meet.

THE LAKE

When Keiko arrived at Ofusa's tea house she found Taichiro standing out on the balcony, ready to leave.

"Good morning. Were you able to sleep?" She came over and leaned on the balcony rail beside him. "You've been waiting for me."

"I was awake early," he said. "The sound of the river made me want to get up and see the sun come over the Eastern Hills."

"As early as that?"

"Yes, but the hills are too close for a real sunrise. The green of the hills brightens, and the Kamo glistens in the morning light."

"Have you been watching all this time?"

"It was interesting to see the streets across the river come alive."

"You couldn't sleep? Didn't you like it here?" Then

she added softly: "I'd be pleased if you were thinking of me, though."

He did not reply.

"You won't tell me?"

"I was thinking of you."

"I made you say that."

"But *you* must have slept well." Taichiro looked at her. Keiko shook her head. "No."

"Your eyes are shining as if you did."

"That's because of you! Missing a night or two of sleep doesn't matter."

Her moist, radiant eyes were fixed on him. He took her hand.

"Such a cold hand," Keiko whispered.

"Yours is warm." He clasped each of her fingers in turn, marveling at their delicacy. They seemed incredibly slender and fragile, as if they could easily be bitten off. He wanted to take them in his mouth. Her fingers suggested a young girl's vulnerability. And here before his very eyes was her lovely profile, the exquisite ears and long, slim neck.

"So you do your painting with these slender fingers." He brought her hand up to his lips. Keiko looked at her hand. There were tears in her eyes.

"Are you sad?"

"I'm too happy! This morning I'd cry at your slightest touch. . . . I feel as if something has ended for me."

"But what?"

"You shouldn't ask me that."

"It hasn't ended, it's begun. Isn't the end of one thing the beginning of another?"

"Yes, but what's done is done, it's entirely different. That's the way a woman feels. She's reborn."

He was about to draw her into his arms when the strength ebbed from his caress. She leaned against him. He gripped the balcony rail.

From the river bank just below them came the shrill barking of a little dog. A neighborhood woman taking her terrier out for a walk had run into a big Akita dog, led by a man who looked like a cook from one of the nearby restaurants. The Akita dog ignored the terrier, but the woman had to crouch and gather her barking, wriggling little dog into her arms. When she turned him away from the big one, the terrier seemed to be barking at the two of them on the balcony. The woman looked up and smiled politely.

Keiko shrank behind him. "I can't stand dogs. If a dog barks at you in the morning, you'll have a bad day." Even after the barking stopped she stayed there clinging lightly to his shoulder. "Taichiro, are you happy to be with me?"

"Of course."

"I wonder if you're as happy as I am. . . . I suppose not, really."

As he was thinking how feminine she sounded, he had a sudden awareness of her fragrant breath on his neck. She seemed to be clinging a little closer to him, so close he could feel the soft warmth of her body. Now Keiko belonged to him. There was nothing baffling about her.

"You didn't realize how much I wanted to see you," she said. "I thought we'd never meet again unless I went to Kamakura. It's strange to be here together like this."

"Very strange."

"I mean, I feel as if we've been together all the time, because I've been thinking about you ever since that day we met. But you forgot about me, didn't you? Until you happened to be coming to Kyoto."

"It's strange for you to say that."

"Really? You remembered me now and then?"

"Not that it wasn't painful."

"But why?"

"It makes me think of your teacher, and of what my mother suffered. I was only a child but it's all in my father's novel, you know. The way she would drop a bowl and burst into tears, or carry me in her arms through the streets at night. She wouldn't even notice that I was crying. She seemed to be getting deaf—in her early twenties!" Taichiro hesitated. "Anyway, that novel is still selling. It's ironic, but the royalties have helped support our family for years. They paid for my education and my sister's marriage."

"What's wrong with that?"

"I'm not complaining, but it does seem odd. I can't help disliking a novel that shows my mother as a crazy, jealous woman. And yet whenever there's a new printing she's the one who stamps each copyright slip with the author's seal. She's just a middle-aged woman sitting there good-naturedly tapping away thousands of times

with the seal, so they can publish more copies of a book
that tells how jealous she was. . . . Maybe it's only an
old memory—things are calm enough at home now. You
might think people would look down on her, but instead
they seem respectful."

"After all she's Mrs. Oki Toshio."

"But then there's your teacher, still unmarried."

"There is."

"I wonder how my parents feel about that. They seem
to forget she ever existed. I hate to think I've been living
on money from the sacrifice of a girl's whole life. . . .
And you tell me you want revenge for her."

"Don't." Keiko leaned her cheek against his neck. "My
revenge is finished. I'm just me."

He turned and put his hands on her shoulders.

Her voice was barely audible. "Miss Ueno said I
needn't come back."

"Why?"

"Because I was going to meet you."

"You told her?"

"Of course."

Taichiro was silent.

"She asked me not to. She said if I went I needn't ever
return."

He let go of her shoulders. The traffic along the opposite bank had picked up, and there were new shades of
green, light and dark, in the Eastern Hills.

"Shouldn't I have told her?" she asked, peering into
his face.

"It's not that," he said stiffly, and began to walk away.

"I seem to be taking revenge on Miss Ueno for my mother."

Keiko followed close behind him. "I never dreamed of that kind of revenge. What a curious thing to say!"

"Shall we go? Or perhaps you ought to go home."

"Don't be cruel."

"This time it's my turn to spoil Miss Ueno's life."

"I'm sorry I talked about revenge last night. Forgive me."

Taichiro hailed a taxi in front of the tea house, and Keiko got in with him. He remained silent as they drove across the city out to the Nisonin Temple in Saga.

Keiko was silent too, except for asking if she could open the window all the way. But she put her hand on his, fondling it gently with her index finger. Her smooth hand was a little damp.

The main gate of the Nisonin Temple was said to have been brought from Hideyoshi's Fushimi Castle in the early seventeenth century. It had the imposing air of a great castle gate.

Keiko remarked that they seemed to be in for another hot day. "This is my first time here," she said.

"I've done a little research on Fujiwara Teika," Taichiro told her. As he climbed the stone steps to the gate he looked around and saw the hem of her kimono rippling as she followed nimbly after him. "We know Teika had a villa on Mt. Ogura called the 'Pavilion of the Autumn Rain,' but people claim three different sites for it. You can't tell which it really was. There's one on the hill behind us, another at a temple not far from here, and then there's the 'Hermitage Away from the Hateful World.'"

"Miss Ueno took me there once."

"Did she? So you've seen the well where they say Teika drew water for his inkstone when he was compiling his anthology of a hundred poets."

"I don't remember seeing that."

"The water is famous—they call it 'willow water.'"

"Did he really use it?"

"Teika was a genius, and all sorts of legends sprang up about him. He was the greatest medieval poet and man of letters."

"Is his tomb here too?"

"No, it's at Shokokuji. But there's a little stone pagoda at the hermitage that is supposed to be a memorial of his cremation." Keiko said no more. Apparently she knew almost nothing of Fujiwara Teika.

Earlier, as their car passed Hirosawa Pond, the view of the beautiful pine-covered hills reflected along the opposite shore had awakened his thoughts of the millennium of history and literature associated with the Saga region. Beyond the low, gently sloping profile of Mt. Ogura he could see Mt. Arashi.

With Keiko beside him, the past seemed all the more alive. He felt that he had indeed come to the ancient capital.

But was not Keiko's impetuousness, the passionate intensity of the girl, softened for him by this setting? Taichiro looked at her.

"Why are you staring at me so oddly?" She seemed a

little abashed, and stretched her hand out to block his gaze. He put his own hand lightly against hers.

"It *is* odd, being here with you. . . . It makes me wonder where I am."

"I wonder too." Keiko dug her nails into her fingers. "And I wonder who this is beside me."

Dense shadows fell on the wide avenue leading up to the temple from the main gate. The avenue was lined with superb red pines interspersed with maples. Even the tips of the pine branches were still. Their trailing shadows played over Keiko's face and her white kimono as she walked along. An occasional maple branch hung low enough to touch.

As they came to the end of the avenue they could see a roofed clay wall at the top of a flight of stone steps. There was the sound of falling water. They climbed the steps and went along the wall to the left. A stream of water was pouring from an opening in the base of the wall near a simple gate.

"It has very few visitors for such a well-known temple." He paused beside her. "Today it seems deserted."

Mt. Ogura lay before them. The copper-roofed main hall of the temple had a quiet dignity.

"See this fine old holly oak," Taichiro said, walking toward it. "People call it the most famous tree in the Western Hills." From top to bottom the oak thrust out gnarled branches, knotty with age, but it was thickly covered with young leaves. Its short branches seemed bursting with energy.

"I've always been fond of this old tree, but it's years

since I looked at it like this." He talked only of the oak tree, not at all of the temple.

As they came back past the Hall of the Goddess Benten he looked up a long, steep flight of stone steps. "Can you climb these in a kimono?" he asked.

Keiko smiled and shook her head. "Not very well." Then she added: "Take my hand. After that you can carry me."

"We'll go slowly."

"Is it up there?"

"Yes. Sanetaka's tomb is at the top of the steps."

"You came to Kyoto just to see that tomb. You didn't come to meet me."

"Exactly." He grasped her hand, but released it. "I'll go on alone. Wait for me here."

"I can do it. You ought to know those steps won't bother me. I don't care *how* far we climb!" She took his hand and began going up with him.

Evidently the worn old steps were seldom used now; weeds and ferns sprouted at the foot of each step. Here and there yellow flowers bloomed.

"Is this it?" Keiko asked as they came to three little stone pagodas standing in a row at one side.

"A little higher," said Taichiro, but he turned in among them. "Beautiful, aren't they? These are the 'Tombs of the Three Emperors'—they're masterpieces of stonework. The one on this side and the five-ringed one in the middle are especially fine, I think."

Keiko nodded, gazing at them.

"The stone has a lovely patina," he went on.

"Are they medieval?"

"Yes, but the one with ten rings over there seems a little later than the others. They say it was a thirteen-ringed pagoda that lost its upper part."

The grace and refinement of the little stone pagodas obviously appealed to Keiko's artistic sense. She seemed to forget that she was standing hand in hand with him.

"None of the tombs of famous people around here can match them."

At the very top of the stone steps they came to the modest Founder's Shrine, which contained only a tall stone tablet inscribed with the achievements of the priest Tanku. Taichiro walked quickly past it to a row of tombstones along its right side. "Here we are. These belong to the Sanjonishi family. The one on the far right is Sanetaka's, where it says 'Lord Sanetaka, Former Chamberlain.'"

Keiko looked and saw a small gravestone, no more than knee-high, flanked by an even smaller stone marker bearing the name of Sanetaka. The two gravestones on its left also had slender markers, with the inscriptions "Lord Kineda, Former Minister of the Right" and "Lord Saneeda, Former Chamberlain."

"Would high officials have such simple-looking monuments?" Keiko asked.

"That's right. I like these plain little stones."

Except for the accompanying name tablets, they were no different from the gravestones of the unknown persons buried at the Nembutsu Temple in Adashino. The stones here were also old, mossy, earth-stained, worn out of shape by time. They were mute. Taichiro crouched beside Sanetaka's gravestone as if he were trying to hear a distant, faint voice from the past. Drawn by his hand, Keiko crouched too.

"Rather appealing, isn't it?" he said. "I'm doing research on Sanetaka. He lived to be eighty-two and kept a diary for over sixty years—it's a great historical source for the sixteenth century. You often find him mentioned in the diaries of other court nobles and poets, too. It was a fascinating period, a time of cultural vitality in the midst of wars and political upheavals."

"Is that why you're fond of his tombstone?"

"I suppose so."

"Have you been studying him for years?"

"Three years. No, it must be four or five by now."

"And your inspiration comes from this tomb?"

"My inspiration? I don't know——" At that moment Keiko let herself topple against him. Still crouching, he rocked back on his heels to steady himself as her weight almost bore him over. Then she was lying across his lap looking up at him, her arms around his neck.

"Right in front of your precious tombstone. . . . Why don't you give *me* some fond memories of it? This stone is where your heart is. That's all it means."

"All it means?" He echoed her words vacantly. "In time even tombstones change."

"What are you saying?"

"It's true there comes a time when a tombstone loses its meaning."

"*What*?"

"You're too close." Now his lips were almost touching her ear.

"Don't! You're tickling." Keiko rubbed her head against his chest and looked up at him out of the corners of her eyes. "You shouldn't tickle me with your breath like that. I hate men who tease."

"I'm not teasing."

On the verge of laughter, he realized for the first time that his arms were around her, supporting her as she lay there across his lap. He was conscious of the weight of her body, and yet of a buoyant softness to it.

Keiko's long kimono sleeves had slipped back, and her bare arms were still around his neck. Suddenly he was also conscious of the cool touch of her smooth, moist skin.

"Teasing your pretty ear, am I?" He tried to calm his breathing.

"I'm sensitive there," she whispered.

Her ears were tempting. Taichiro fingered them gently. She kept her eyes wide open and did not move.

"Like mysterious flowers," he said, toying with her ears.

"Are they?"

"Can you hear anything?"

"Of course. Something like——"

"Like what?"

"I wonder. Like a bee hovering in a flower . . . or maybe a butterfly."

"It's because I'm touching them."

"Do you enjoy touching a woman's ears?"

His hands froze.

"Do you?" she repeated softly.

"I've never seen such beautiful ones," he said at last.

"I like to clean out people's ears for them," said Keiko. "Odd, isn't it? I've become quite an expert. Shall I do it for you some time?"

Taichiro did not answer.

"There isn't a breath of air," she went on.

"No, only a sunlit world."

"I'll always remember being in your arms in front of an old tomb on a morning like this. It seems strange for a tomb to create a memory."

"But they're built for memories, aren't they?"

"I'm sure *your* memory of this morning will soon vanish." She made an effort to lift herself from his lap. "It's too painful!"

"Why do you think I won't remember?"

"It's too painful for me, being like this!"

As she tried to free herself Taichiro held her closer. He brushed his lips against hers.

"No, no!"

He was startled by her fierce refusal. As if to hide her lips, she pressed her face tight against his chest. He ran his hand over her hair, around to her forehead, and tried to tilt back her face. She resisted.

"You're hurting my eye!" she exclaimed, yielding. Her eyes were closed.

"Which one?"

"The right."

"Does it still hurt?"

"I think so. Don't you see tears?"

There was no sign of irritation on the eyelid. Bending down automatically, he kissed her eye.

Keiko sighed but did not resist.

He could feel her long lashes between his lips. Suddenly uneasy, he drew back. "You don't mind? Though you won't let me kiss your mouth?"

"I don't know! How can you talk like that?" She scrambled to her feet, almost knocking him over. Her white handbag was on the ground. Taichiro picked it up, rose, and gave it to her.

"Your bag seems awfully large."

"I have a bathing suit in it."

"A bathing suit?"

"You promised to go to Lake Biwa, you know." Keiko took out a mirror and peered at her right eye, and rubbed the eyelid. Noticing his steady gaze, she flushed and looked down with bewitching shyness. For a moment she ran her fingertips over his white shirt, where there was a trace of her lipstick.

"What shall we do?" he said, taking her hand.

"I'm sorry, it won't come off."

"I'm not worried about my shirt. I mean, what shall we do now?"

"I don't know!" Keiko tilted her head. "I haven't the least idea."

"We can go to the lake this afternoon, can't we?"

"What time is it?"

"A quarter to ten."

"So early? The way the sunlight filters down, it looks

like noon." Keiko glanced around through the trees. "That must be Mt. Arashi over there. I should think people would come here in the summer too."

"Even if they visit the temple they're not likely to climb this far." He mopped his face with a handkerchief, feeling somewhat relieved to be talking casually with her again. "Would you like to see where they say the Pavilion of the Autumn Rain used to be? I've been here two or three times before, but I've never gone all the way up."

A wooden guidepost pointing toward the site stood at the base of the slope behind them.

"Are we climbing some more?" She looked up the mountain. "I don't care how high it is. If it's hard walking, I can go barefoot."

The path threaded upward through dense woods. Taichiro heard the twigs brushing her kimono, and turned to take her hand.

Soon they came to a fork in the path.

"Probably we should go to the left," he said, hesitating. "It looks a bit dangerous." The path ran along the edge of a cliff.

"I'm afraid I'd slip," said Keiko, clinging to his arm. "Let's take the one to the right."

"We might as well. It seems to go to the top of the mountain."

This branch of the path was almost hidden by low trees. Taichiro let Keiko lead him along it, but suddenly she stopped. "Do I have to go through a thicket, dressed like this?"

Beyond them stood three tall pines. Through the

pines they could see the Northern Hills and, below, the outskirts of the city. "I wonder where that could be," said Taichiro, as Keiko leaned against him.

"I have no idea." Slowly she slumped over into his arms. He staggered, and let himself be borne to the ground under her weight. As they lay there together she reached down and smoothed her skirt.

When he moved his lips toward her eyes Keiko merely closed her eyelids. Even when he kissed her on the mouth she made no attempt to avoid him. But she kept her lips tightly pressed together.

Taichiro caressed her slender young neck and began to slip his hand under her kimono.

"Don't do that!" Keiko clutched his hand in hers. Then he slid his palm down over her kimono against the swell of her right breast, his hand still covered by both of hers, but she guided it across to the other breast. She opened her eyes narrowly and looked up at him. "You mustn't touch the right one. I don't like it."

"Oh?" Mystified, he let his hand fall from her left breast.

Keiko's eyes were still narrowed. "The right one makes me feel sad."

"Sad?"

"Yes."

"But why?"

"I don't know. Maybe because my heart isn't on that side." She closed her eyes shyly and nestled closer, her left breast against him. "Maybe there's something defec-

tive about a girl's body. Even losing that defect may make
her feel sad.''

Taichiro felt an appealing stimulation when she told
him there was something defective about a girl's body.
Yet the way Keiko had talked just now seemed to him to
prove that it was not the first time she had let a man
touch her breasts. That tempted him too. Grasping her
firmly by her hair, he kissed her. Her forehead and neck
were bathed in perspiration.

The two walked downhill, past the graves of the
Suminokura family, to the Gio Temple. From there they
turned back and strolled as far as Mt. Arashi.

They had lunch at the Kitcho restaurant.

Afterward the waitress came in and told them their car
had arrived.

Somewhat taken aback, Taichiro looked at Keiko.
While he had thought she was in the powder room she
must have paid the bill and hired a car for them.

As they were driving through Kyoto near the Nijo
Castle Keiko remarked: "I didn't realize we could get
there in such a short time.''

"Get where?''

"Don't be so absent-minded! Lake Biwa, of course.''

The car headed toward the tall pagoda of the Eastern
Temple, passed Kyoto Station, and went on by the temple. They were circling through the southern part of the
city. For a time they followed the Kamo River, a rough

stretch, rather than its usual placid course. The driver told them the mountain that lay ahead was called Mt. Ushio, meaning "oxtail." Skirting to the left of it, they crossed the Eastern Hills.

The view of the lake spread out below them.

"That's Lake Biwa!" Keiko declared briskly. "So I've finally brought you here."

Taichiro was surprised to see how many boats were out—sailboats, motorboats, sightseeing boats.

They drove down to the old town of Otsu. Not far from the observation point overlooking the lake, they veered off to the left, passed a place where motorboats were racing, went through Hama-Otsu, and turned into the tree-lined driveway of the Lake Biwa Hotel. Automobiles were parked along both sides.

Taichiro was startled to think that Keiko must have given the hotel as their destination when she hired the car.

A hotel attendant came out to open the car door. There was nothing to do but go in.

Without a glance at Taichiro, Keiko went straight up to the front desk and asked: "Do you have a reservation for Oki, from Kitcho's at Mt. Arashi?"

"Yes, indeed," the room clerk replied. "For one night, I believe."

Then she stepped back to have Taichiro sign the registration card. After what she had said, he felt obliged to give his real name and address. Adding the words "and Keiko" to his own name somehow made him breathe more easily.

The boy with the room key showed them into the elevator but only took them up to the next floor.

Keiko seemed pleased with the suite.

Besides an inner bedroom, there was a large room looking out on the lake along one side and on the hills bordering Kyoto along another. Perhaps to match the hotel's Momoyama-style gabled architecture, the balcony outside was enclosed with a red balustrade. The low-paneled walls and sliding windows, the thick-framed glass doors, all had a dignified, old-fashioned air. Each of the wide windows covered a whole wall.

Soon a maid brought green tea.

Keiko stood motionless at the window by the lake, holding the edge of the white lace curtains with both hands.

Taichiro sat in the middle of the sofa, watching her. She was wearing a different kimono from yesterday's, but the same rainbow obi.

The lake stretched out on her left. Clusters of sailboats were tacking along together. Most of the sails were white, but a few were red or purple or dark blue. Here and there motorboats dashed about casting up spray and trailing wakes of foam.

Through the window came the sound of motorboat engines, of voices from the hotel pool, of a lawn mower somewhere. Inside there was the hum of the airconditioner.

For a time he waited for her to speak. Then he asked if she wanted a cup of tea.

She shook her head. "Why don't you talk?" she said.

"Why are you so silent? It's cruel of you!" She tugged at the curtains petulantly. "Don't you think it's a beautiful view?"

"Yes, it's beautiful. But I was thinking how beautiful *you* are. The nape of your neck, your obi . . . "

"Thinking of me in your arms at the temple?"

"Thinking of—that?"

"I suppose you're angry with me. You're shocked. I can tell."

"Perhaps I am."

"I'm shocked too. It's fearful when a woman gives herself completely." She lowered her voice. "So that's why you won't come here beside me?"

Taichiro got up and went to her. He put his hand on her shoulder, guiding her gently over to the sofa. She sat close to him but kept her eyes down. "Let me have some tea," she whispered. He picked up the cup and held it out to her. "From your mouth."

He took some tea in his mouth and let it seep little by little between her lips. Eyes closed, head tilted back, Keiko sipped the tea. Except for her lips and throat, she was inert.

"More," she said, still not moving. Taichiro took another mouthful of tea, and gave it to her mouth-to-mouth. "Ah, that was good." Keiko opened her eyes. "I could die now. If only it had been poison. . . . I'm done for. Done for. And so are you." Then she said:

"Turn the other way." Pushing him halfway round, she pressed her face against his shoulder. She put her arms around him, and searched for his hands. Taichiro grasped one of her hands in his, gazing at it as he stroked each of her fingers in turn.

"I'm sorry," Keiko said. "How thoughtless of me. You'd probably like a bath. Suppose I draw the water."

"All right."

"Unless you'd rather just have a shower."

"Do I need one?"

"I like you this way. I've never known a smell I liked so much." She paused. "But you must want to feel re-freshed."

Keiko disappeared into the bedroom. He could hear water running in the bathroom beyond it.

As he watched an excursion steamer nearing the hotel pier, Keiko came to tell him the bath was ready.

Taichiro gave his body, sweaty since Saga, a thorough lathering.

A sudden knock on the bathroom door made him shrink back. Was Keiko coming in? Then he heard her say that he was wanted on the telephone.

"It couldn't be for me. Who's calling? . . . There must be some mistake."

"It's for you," she repeated.

"That's funny. No one knows I'm here."

"But it *is* for you."

Without stopping to dry himself, Taichiro slipped on a bath kimono and went out. "You say it's for me?" he asked suspiciously.

There was a telephone on the night table between the two beds. He was just going over to it, when Keiko told him to come to the other room.

On a little table beside the television set was a telephone with the receiver off its cradle. As Taichiro picked up the receiver and held it to his ear, Keiko said: "It's from your home, from Kamakura."

"It is?" he exclaimed, paling. "Why on earth?"

"Your mother is on the line." Then she added in a strained voice: "I called her. I said I'm here at the Lake Biwa Hotel, and you've promised to marry me. I said I hoped she'd give us her consent."

Taichiro stared at her.

Of course his mother could hear what Keiko had just said. When he went to take a bath he had closed the bedroom and bathroom doors; what with the water splashing, he would not have heard Keiko make the telephone call. Had urging him to bathe been part of her plan?

"Taichiro? Is Taichiro there?" His mother's voice vibrated through the receiver clenched in his hand.

As he stared at her, Keiko returned his stare, unblinking. Her beautiful eyes had a piercing radiance.

"Isn't Taichiro there?"

"Yes, Mother, I'm here," he said, putting the receiver to his ear.

"It *is* you, Taichiro, isn't it?" Her voice quavered. "Don't do it! Taichiro, please don't."

He did not reply.

"That girl—you know what kind she is, don't you? You must know."

Again Taichiro said nothing. Keiko put her arms around him from behind. Nudging the receiver aside with her cheek, she pressed her lips close to his ear. "Mother," she called softly. "Mother, I wonder if you realize why I phoned you."

"Taichiro, can you hear me?" his mother asked. "Who's there?"

"I am," he said, drawing away from Keiko's lips and thrusting the receiver back to his ear.

"Such impudence, talking on the phone ahead of you! Did she have you call?" His mother did not wait for an answer. "Taichiro, come home! Leave that hotel at once and come home. . . . She's listening in, isn't she? I don't care! I want her to hear. Taichiro, don't have anything to do with that girl. She's a dreadful person—I know! I can't stand being tortured again. This time it would kill me! I'm not just saying that because she's Miss Ueno's pupil."

As he listened, Keiko's lips were touching the back of his neck. "If I hadn't been Miss Ueno's pupil I'd never have met you," she whispered.

"It's because she's spiteful," his mother went on. "I think she tried to seduce your father too!"

"Oh?" he said faintly, and turned to look at Keiko. Her head moved with his, her lips still clinging to his neck. He felt that he was insulting his mother by listening to her over the telephone as Keiko kissed him. Yet he could not simply hang up. "We can talk about it when I come home."

"Yes—come home right away! You haven't done anything wrong with her, have you? You can't mean to stay overnight?" There was no reply. "Taichiro, look into her eyes! Think about what she says. Why do you suppose she wants to marry you, when she's Miss Ueno's pupil? It's an evil woman's scheme. At least she's evil as far as we're concerned. I'm sure of that, it's not just my imagination. I had a feeling it was bad luck for you to go to Kyoto this time and I was right! Your father worried too, and said it looked suspicious. Taichiro, if you won't come home we're both going to take the next flight to Kyoto."

"I understand."

"You understand *what*?" Then, to make sure: "You're coming home, aren't you? You're really coming home?"

"All right."

Keiko darted off into the bedroom and shut the door.

Taichiro stood quietly by the window, gazing out at the lake. A light plane, probably for sightseeing, curved away low over the water. Some of the motorboats were bounding along at high speed, one of them towing a girl on water skis.

He could hear voices from the pool. Three young women in bathing suits were lying sprawled provocatively on the grass below his window.

He heard Keiko calling him from the bedroom. When he opened the door she was standing there in a white bathing suit. He caught his breath, and looked away. Her slightly tanned skin glistened so dazzlingly that he hardly noticed the white wool suit.

"It's beautiful," she said, going over to the window. The suit left her whole back bare. "See how beautiful the sky is, there by the mountains."

Sharply etched golden rays of sunlight slanted down over the mountain. "Isn't that Mt. Hiei?" Taichiro asked.

"Yes. It makes me think of spears stabbing through our fate. And what about your mother?" She turned to him. "I want her to come here, your father too."

"Don't be absurd."

"I do! I'm serious." Suddenly Keiko clung to him. "Come swimming with me. I want to be in cold, cold water. You promised, you know. You promised to go for a motorboat ride too. That's been a promise ever since you came." She nestled against him, letting his body support her. "Are you going back to Kamakura because you talked to your mother? You'll find they've come here. Probably your father won't want to, but your mother will see to it."

"Keiko, did you seduce him?"

Her face against his chest, she shook her head. "Did I seduce you? Did I?"

His arms were around her bare back. "I'm not talking about myself. Don't change the subject."

"Don't *you* change it! I'm asking if I seduced you. Is that what you think?" She paused. "How can a man be so cruel to a girl he's holding in his arms, asking her if she seduced his father?" Keiko started to weep. "'What do you want me to say? I think I'll drown myself. . . . "

As he gripped her trembling shoulders he felt one of the shoulder straps under his hand. He began slipping it down, exposing her breast halfway, and then slipped off the other strap. Keiko lurched against him, arching her back, her naked breasts thrust forward. "Don't! Not the right one. Please! Please, not the right one!" Tears were streaming from her tight-shut eyes.

Keiko draped a large towel around her shoulders before going out to swim. Taichiro was in his shirt-sleeves. Together they went down past the lobby to the garden facing the lake. A tall tree in front of them was blooming with white flowers that looked like hibiscus.

There were swimming pools on both sides of the garden. Children were using the one set in the lawn on the right. The pool on the left was fenced in, on a slight elevation at the edge of the lawn.

Taichiro stopped at the gate to the swimming pool on the left.

"Aren't you coming?" Keiko asked.

"No, I'll wait for you." He felt a little self-conscious being with a girl who attracted so much attention.

"Oh? I'd just like a quick dip," she said. "It's my first this year, and I want to see how I do."

Weeping willows and cherry trees stood at intervals on the lawn along the shore.

Taichiro sat down on the bench in the shade of an old elm and looked toward the pool. He could not see Keiko until she was standing on the low diving board, poised to dive. Keiko's taut body was silhouetted against Lake Biwa and the distant mountains. The mountains were veiled in mist. A faint, elusive pink tinged the darkening waters of the lake. By now the yacht sails reflected the tranquil colors of evening. Keiko dived in, sending up a cloud of spray.

After Keiko left the pool she rented a motorboat and asked Taichiro to come for a ride.

"It's getting dark," he said. "Why not go tomorrow?"

"Tomorrow?" Her eyes lighted up. "Then you'll stay? You'll really stay? . . . I don't know about tomorrow. Isn't that so? Anyway, just keep this one promise. We'll come right back. For a little while I want to be out on the water with you. I want us to cut through our fate and drift along on the waves. Tomorrow always escapes us. Let's go today." She pulled him by the arm. "See how many boats are still out!"

Three hours later Ueno Otoko heard of the motorboat accident on Lake Biwa over the radio and rushed by car to the hotel. She had learned from the news report that a girl named Keiko had been picked up by one of the sailboats. Keiko was in bed when she arrived.

As Otoko came into the bedroom she asked the maid in attendance whether Keiko was still unconscious.

"She's under a sedative," the maid replied.

"Then she's out of danger?"

"The doctor said there's nothing to worry about. She looked dead when they brought her ashore, but they gave her artificial respiration and soon revived her. She began thrashing around furiously, calling the name of the man who was with her."

"How is he?"

"They haven't found him yet, in spite of all the people looking for him."

"They haven't?" There was a tremor in Otoko's voice. She went back to the other room and looked out at the lake. The lights of motorboats were circling restlessly over the black sheet of water stretching far to the left of the hotel.

"All the motorboats around here are out, not just ours," the maid called to her. "The police boats are out too, and they've made bonfires along the shore. But it's probably too late to save him."

Otoko gripped the window curtain.

Away from the uneasily stirring lights of the motorboats, an excursion steamer festooned with red lanterns moved slowly toward the hotel pier. Fireworks could be seen shooting up from the opposite bank.

Otoko noticed that her knees were trembling. Then her whole body began to tremble and the steamer's lanterns seemed to be swaying. With an effort, she turned away. The bedroom door was open. Keiko's bed caught her eye, and she hurried back into the bedroom as if forgetting she had been there before.

Keiko was sleeping peacefully. Her breathing was calm.

Otoko became all the more uneasy. "Can we leave her like this?"

The maid nodded.

"When will she wake up?"

"I don't know."

Otoko put her hand against Keiko's forehead. The cool, damp skin felt sticky. Keiko's face was drained of color except for a faint redness in the cheeks.

Her hair lay spread out over her pillow in a tangled mass, so black that it still looked wet. There was a glimpse of her lovely teeth between parted lips. Both arms were at her side under the blanket. As she lay there, head turned straight up, Keiko's pure, innocent sleeping face touched Otoko deeply. Her face seemed to be bidding farewell, to Otoko and to life.

Otoko was reaching out to shake her into consciousness when she heard a knock at the door of the other room. The maid went to open the door.

Oki Toshio and his wife came in. As soon as he saw Otoko he stopped.

"So you're Miss Ueno," said Fumiko.

It was their first meeting.

"So you're the one who had my son killed." Her voice was quiet and emotionless.

Otoko began to move her lips, but no words came out. She was leaning over Keiko's bed, propping herself up with one arm. Fumiko came toward her. Otoko shrank away.

Fumiko grasped the front of Keiko's night kimono with both hands and shook her. "Wake up! Wake up!" As she shook her harder and harder Keiko's head rocked back and forth. "Why don't you wake up?"

"It's no use," Otoko told her. "She's under sedation."

"I have to ask her something." Fumiko was still trying to rouse her. "It's a matter of life or death for my son!"

"Let's wait a while," said Oki. "All those people out there are looking for him." He put his arm around her shoulder, and they left the room.

With a sigh, Otoko sank down on the bed, staring at Keiko's sleeping face. Tears were trickling from the corners of Keiko's eyes.

"Keiko!"

Keiko opened her eyes. Tears were still sparkling in them as she looked up at Otoko.

About the Author

Yasunari Kawabata, winner of the 1968 Nobel Prize for Literature, was one of Japan's most distinguished novelists. He was famous for adding to the once fashionable naturalism imported from France a sensual, more Japanese impressionism. Born in Osaka in 1899, he hoped as a boy to become a painter—an aspiration reflected in his novels—but his first stories were published while he was still in high school, and he decided to become a writer.

He was graduated from Tokyo Imperial University in 1924. His story "The Izu Dancer," first published in 1925, appeared in *The Atlantic Monthly* in 1955. It captures the shy eroticism of adolescence, and from that time Kawabata devoted his novels largely to aspects of love. Three of his major works published in the United States fall into this category: *Snow Country* (1956), *Thousand Cranes* (1959), and *The Sound of the Mountain* (1970). *The Master of* Go (1972) is an elegiac, poignant, and symbolic novel about the defeat of a traditional grand master of Japanese chess by a younger, more modern-minded challenger.

Kawabata was found dead, by his own hand, on the evening of April 16, 1972. He left no suicide note, and no satisfactory explanation for his suicide has been offered.

About the Translator

Howard Scott Hibbett took his doctorate in Japanese literature at Harvard. He has lived in Japan at various times, has taught at the University of California, and is now Professor of Japanese Literature at Harvard. Among other Japanese fiction, he has translated *The Key* and *Diary of a Mad Old Man* by Junichiro Tanizaki.

A Note on the Type

This book was set on the computer in Baskerville, a type face originally designed by John Baskerville (1706-75). Baskerville, a writing master in Birmingham, England, began experimenting about 1750 with type design and punch cutting. His first book, set throughout in his new types, was a Virgil in royal quarto, published in 1757, and it was followed by other famous editions from his press. Baskerville's types, which are distinctive and elegant in design, were a forerunner of what we know today as the "modern" group of type faces.

This book was composed by CompuComp Corp., New York, New York, printed and bound by The Haddon Craftsmen, Inc., Scranton, Pennsylvania, and designed by Anthea Lingeman.